The storm raged on outside the house

David fascinated Felicity by talking about the places he'd been, the people he'd met. But exhaustion took hold eventually and she interrupted confessing, "I'll have to go to bed now."

"Do you want me to leave?" he asked.

It was stormy outside, and she doubted her ability to send him away. "I'd like you to stay, but you'll have to sleep in the chair."

"The chair will do fine," he said.

Felicity curled up on the divan, and David turned out the lamp. "Is the chair all right?" she called softly.

"Adequate."

"Does adequate mean all right?" she persisted.

"Am I being obtuse?" he asked silkily. "Have you changed you~

"About what?"

"Be quiet and go t~
to join you?"

D1410190

JANE DONNELLY
is also the author of these
Harlequin Romances

Call Up
the Storm

Jane Donnelly

Harlequin Books

TORONTO • NEW YORK • LOS ANGELES • LONDON
AMSTERDAM • PARIS • SYDNEY • HAMBURG
STOCKHOLM • ATHENS • TOKYO • MILAN

Original hardcover edition published in 1983
by Mills & Boon Limited

ISBN 0-373-02552-1

Harlequin Romance first edition June 1983

CHAPTER ONE

FELICITY MAYNE would have been happier if the sun had been shining. When it was the rugged Cornish coastline of Tregorran Cove had artists and bird-watchers drooling, but today the sky was black and the sea was a dark sullen green. The stone slate-roofed cottages edging the small harbour, between towering cliffs, all had their doors closed against the steady downpour of rain, and the only bright spot was Felicity herself, in scarlet mac and wellingtons, hurrying across the causeway.

She had been keeping a watch for the white Renault for the last couple of hours. There wasn't much traffic on a day like this, and as soon as she spotted the car, coming down the steep road from the cliff top, she hurried to meet it.

The car stopped by the sea wall, overlooking a rocky deserted beach, but no one got out. No one came out of the houses either. This wasn't a popular holiday resort, even at the height of the summer. Fishermen lived here, a few of the houses took in bed and breakfast tourists, but it was a tiny village, with a general store-cum-post office half way up the hill. Usually there was someone around, but today's weather was foul, and Felicity felt it was a grim start to the holiday that was supposed to be averting Deirdre's nervous breakdown.

When Felicity had invited her it had seemed a natural thing to do. They had been friends at boarding school, and now Deirdre was at the end of her tether and of course Felicity wanted to help. 'You come here,' she had urged. 'Come right away and stay as long as you like. It's beautiful here,' and Deirdre had said, 'Yes, it is, isn't it? I remember.'

But Deirdre was remembering holidays from school nearly five years ago. The weather hadn't bothered them then, and looking back it seemed to Felicity that for most of those holidays the sun had shone.

She crunched over the shingle, climbed the rock steps and ran, slightly encumbered by her gumboots, towards the solitary car. She would have preferred to be sitting on the harbour wall, all smiles, with a few friendly neighbours around. But as soon as she got Deirdre inside the house there would be a warm welcome for her.

Deirdre Osborne was slumped in the driving seat, and when Felicity tapped on the window she opened the door and smiled wanly, 'Well, I made it.'

'It's lovely to see you,' said Felicity.

It was a long time since they had met, although their Christmas cards always had the message 'We really must get together next year' under the scribbled notes of this year's news. Felicity knew that Deirdre had taken a course in business studies when she left school, had various jobs and was now working as secretary for an advertising company. She had a flat in London and what sounded like a full and lively life.

But a few days ago Felicity had come across an old birthday book at the bottom of a drawer, realised that Deirdre's birthday was due, and sent her a card—one of the cheerful silly sort, designed to raise a quick grin. By return came a letter that had her dashing to the boatyard phone to ring Deirdre's flat.

When Deirdre answered Felicity had sagged with relief, because the letter had sounded suicidal, and a few minutes' conversation confirmed that Deirdre was in black depression.

Man trouble! When Felicity tried reassurance, 'I'm so sorry, but it happens, doesn't it, to all of us, and we all get over it,' Deirdre asked, 'Has it ever happened to you like this?' and Felicity couldn't honestly answer, 'Yes.'

She had fancied men who were not for her, one had moved on who she would rather had stayed, but she had never come within a mile of pouring pills into a multi-coloured heap and considering the darkness they would bring.

In her letter Deirdre said she had done just that the night before, then waited for the morning post to see if her lover had remembered her birthday. He hadn't, but there had been Felicity's card. On the outside it had read, 'Getting you down, is it, the way the years are rolling on?' Felicity was a few weeks older than Deirdre, she had just had her twenty-second birthday. Inside it said, 'Hang on, the future isn't so bad,' and a cavorting crone was waving a glass of champagne. With a touch of white and black paint Felicity had changed the face into a grinning caricature of her own. It was not a card she would have chosen if she had known the circumstances, but it had made Deirdre get out pen and paper and spill out her troubles to her old school friend.

Deirdre would have friends around, of course, but when Felicity phoned she told her she had realised that she had to get right away, and Felicity said, 'You come here.' That was yesterday. Today she was here, the rain beating on her car and bouncing off the stone-flagged seafront.

Felicity was carrying an umbrella which she waved towards a gap between the houses. 'Remember the boatyard? We're still parking there. Then I'm afraid we'll have to run for it.'

She closed the car door and Deirdre backed and turned while Felicity followed the Renault into the yard, between the dinghies and the coils of ropes and lobster pots and the general mêlée of fishermen's equipment. One wall had parking bays marked out beneath, and a notice 'Private parking for Gull Rock House'. There was room for half a dozen cars and one space was taken; Deirdre drew up alongside a blue Metro with a flight of gulls painted across it and opened her car door again as Felicity reached her.

'This,' said Felicity, pulling a face as the rain dripped off her chin, 'is doing my business no good at all. When I'm rich I'm going to have the causeway reinforced and make it good and wide. It puts them off, having to leave their cars and walk.'

'Well, it would,' Deirdre agreed. 'Do you ever get anybody staying?'

'Of *course* I do—I've got a family in now.'

This was only Felicity's first season in running a very small hotel and she hadn't expected it to be an immediate and roaring success, but she felt quite peeved at the suggestion that she had had no customers. Deirdre was an invited guest, but much more of this, thought Felicity mischievously, and I'll present you with a bill when you leave!

She wouldn't, of course. That would be a joke in very bad taste, and humour never had been Deirdre's strong point. Right now she seemed in no state to see the funny side of anything, but she hadn't changed much in looks in the three years since they had met in London for lunch one day.

She had always been quite beautiful, with dark thick hair waving from a centre parting, and a pale oval Madonna face. A tall willowy girl in a grey silk blouse and grey cord jeans, wearing an assortment of long thin gold chains, she was hardly dressed for running across the beach to the house built on the rocks out in the bay.

There was a large case on the back seat and as Deirdre reached for the blond cashmere coat lying on top Felicity asked, 'Haven't you got a mac? You're going to ruin that.'

Felicity shrugged, 'It doesn't matter.'

'Don't be silly. It's a beautiful coat.' Deirdre always had had beautiful things. Her parents had separated before she came to boarding school at the age of eleven. They sent her extravagant presents but never came to see her, and when she did go 'home' for the holidays it was to other relatives or friends of her parents, where she couldn't have been happy because she would come back eagerly to school, as though her real family was there.

She was the only girl in the dormitory with a silver-backed hairbrush, who wore silk undies under the regulation uniform, but nobody envied her. Most of her schooldays had passed under Felicity's shadow and Felicity's protection.

Felicity had vitality. She was not a leader so much as an individual. On their first night at school, when the four new girls were settling down in their little white-counterpaned beds, Felicity had produced a shell and sat with it pressed to her ear, listening.

'What are you doing?' Deirdre had asked.

'Listening to the sea.' She held the spiral whelk shell in her cupped hands, a small girl with a pointed face and huge tip-tilted eyes, green as deep sea water, offering it to Deirdre. 'You listen, you'll hear it.'

They all did. She was convincing because she could hear it herself, because she was lonely for the sea. Her grandfather had packed the shell in her case and this was the first night apart from holidays, that Felicity had slept without the sound of the waves lulling her to sleep.

'You come from Cornwall, don't you?' said one of the new girls.

'Oh yes.' Lights had been turned out, except for one lamp, and Felicity's smooth straight fair hair falling around her face gleamed in the lamplight. 'My great-great-grandmother was a sea-witch,' she said, and Ann and Emily giggled nervously.

'You're having us on, there's no such thing as witches,' said Emily, a child with a logical mind who would later major in pure maths.

'Aren't there?' said Felicity. 'Well, she was washed up in a storm and nobody ever knew for sure where she came from, and she could cast spells, and she was my great-great-grandmother.' She laughed too, a throaty chuckle, and the other three new girls cheered up, feeling that here was somebody who wasn't going to let the system get her down.

In fact Felicity was probably more homesick than any of them at first. She had pleaded against being sent away to school, but, when her grandmother and mother were killed in a car crash eighteen months before, her grandfather had decided, after much soul-searching, that it would be in the child's best interests.

Looking back, she had enjoyed her schooldays. Unlike Deirdre she had never doubted for a moment that she was loved. She hadn't been sent away to get her out of the way. Every week her grandfather's letter had arrived, and every holiday she came back home to Tregorran Cove, sometimes bringing friends who were always welcomed and who always fell under the strange enchantment of that wild coastline.

But right now the rain was drenching Deirdre, and Felicity handed her the umbrella and lugged the case off the back seat, then took the keys from the ignition and locked the car. Deirdre stood shivering, saying through chattering teeth, 'If I catch pneumonia that could be the end of my troubles.'

'Well, you're not catching it here,' said Felicity briskly, recognising again an echo of her long-ago attitude to Deirdre. Deirdre had never shown much common sense. Her nickname at school, based on her initials and her personality, had been the Dreamy Owl, and although she was now stunningly attractive, and presumably holding down a demanding job, this unhappy love affair seemed to have regressed her back to her schooldays.

Felicity picked up her case. Deirdre was a head taller than Felicity, but Felicity knew every step across the causeway, and they would get along faster if she carried the case. A bearded man, wearing oilskins, passed them as they came out of the boatyard. 'Filthy weather,' he said, grinning broadly.

'The wind's changed,' said Felicity, and Deirdre with her umbrella well down over her head muttered, 'I'm glad to see somebody around, I was beginning to wonder if this had become a ghost town!'

After London Tregorran Cove must seem desolate if you were lonely and unhappy, especially on a day like this when the only sign of life was the seabirds. Felicity quickened her pace, hurrying ahead of Deirdre over the shingle and on to the causeway towards the two-storey house out in the bay.

The house was built of rock, on rocks that could become an islet when storms lashed the coast or tides were high. Usually there was a safe pathway from the beach, although the back of the house overlooked deep water. When it was first built in the early eighteenth century it had stood on the mainland, but over the years the sea had encroached on the shore. Other houses and cottages had slipped beneath the waves, but high on the rocks Gull Rock House had weathered every storm.

Felicity's family had always lived here. The men had been sailors, and the women who loved them had waited for them. Even Felicity's mother, whose husband was lost at sea a month before Felicity was born, had always seemed to be waiting, until the dreadful day of the car crash. After that it had just been Felicity and her grandfather; they were the last of the line, and Felicity was not waiting for anybody.

She believed in herself. She was a small girl, but she had always been robustly healthy, full of life and the gift of laughter.

Behind her, on the causeway, Deirdre said in wonder, 'You haven't really opened a guest-house, have you?'

'Yes, I have—I told you. See, I've got a sign up.'

The name was painted, in white letters on the grey weathered stone, 'Gull Rock House.' There were three wide steps cut in the rock leading to the studded oak door, and Deirdre asked, 'But how are you managing?'

'This is our first season,' said Felicity.

'It was a lovely house.' Deirdre's voice was wistful now. 'I hope you haven't spoiled it, letting strangers in.'

The door opened as they reached the steps and Deirdre gave a little cry of recognition. 'Mrs Clemo!'

'Hello, my dearie.' The woman spoke with a soft Cornish burr, beaming with welcome. She was tall and big-boned, with greying hair taken back in a bun. She held the door wide and the two girls hurried in, rain dripping from them on to the red flagstones.

'My,' said Mrs Cleo, 'you've grown into a rare beauty!'

Deirdre smiled faintly, 'Thank you.' She had been a schoolgirl the last time she came here and her promise of beauty then had been fulfilled. Model girl height, she made Felicity look even shorter than her five foot nothing, and seeing them together Mrs Clemo chuckled, 'As the Captain used to say, this one stopped growing as soon as she could see over the top of the table!'

Felicity's smallness had been an affectionate joke because her grandfather had been a big man. They had teased each other, treating each other as equals almost from her earliest days. Her grandfather had been the first to realise that Felicity had a quick and retentive mind. He was as proud of her cleverness as he was of her looks.

The big room showed little change to Deirdre, except for a bar in one corner, and the addition of several more chintz-covered armchairs. Logs burned in the open fireplace, and in front of the fire a large black labrador was stretched out on a rug. 'Sam?' said Deirdre.

The dog got slowly to its feet and ambled over. 'Dear old Sam!' she gave him a hug which he accepted with amiable condescension, then he returned to the fire and Deirdre looked at the wooden armchair. 'I can't believe your grandfather won't be sitting there,' she said. 'He was a wonderful old man. Don't you miss him?'

'I miss him,' said Felicity.

It was strange about that empty chair. It stood where it always had, beside the hearth, but it was usually the last chair in the room to be taken. Perhaps that was because the other seats all looked more comfortable, but Felicity noticed that her paying guests sat around on sofas and squashy armchairs most of the time while the big polished-wood chair stayed austerely empty.

When somebody did sit on it they seemed awkward and out of place. Only last month Mrs Clemo's daughter, Jessie Tregeagle, had come giggling into the kitchen with a tray of empty coffee cups. 'That little sandy chap's sitting in the Captain's chair. It's a scream, he doesn't half fill it—he's fairly rolling around!'

Rachel Clemo didn't believe in ridiculing the customers. She was almost as anxious for Gull Rock House to succeed as Felicity herself, and she didn't grin as Felicity did. 'That party's taking three bedrooms,' she reminded the younger women, 'and six customers are no laughing matter.'

'Bless them all,' said Felicity. 'Shove a cushion behind him.'

The house, like the chair, had seemed dreadfully empty after her grandfather died. It was a biggish house, but while he lived every room had seemed full and warm and happy.

At twenty-one Felicity was working in a rather smart art gallery, in a busy seaside town about five miles away. She was good at languages and a persuasive salesgirl, and some of the items she sold were her own creations. She enjoyed the work and the possibility that Gordon Stretton—whose family owned the gallery— was falling in love with her. But after the night when her grandfather died in his sleep everything changed.

Her home became a cold and lonely place, and yet she couldn't leave it. She couldn't afford the upkeep. She couldn't face the thought of coming back from work every night and finding it empty. But the idea of putting it up for sale was unbearable.

She sat huddled in the great oak chair, with Sam at her feet. Gordon wanted her to leave here and take a flat or a cottage nearer his home, near the gallery. If she played her cards right he would be asking her to marry him before long. But what she wanted to do was stay here, in this house. Sam looked up at her with pleading eyes, sensing her distress, missing his master, and she stroked his head and whispered, 'It'll be all right, you'll see.'

She had to bring the house to life again, fill it with voices and laughter, or over the years it would fill with ghosts and memories. Neighbours would be calling, of course. In Tregorran Cove everybody knew everybody, and she had friends who would come and visit her. Guests. *Paying guests*! she thought, and shot upright in the chair. Why not paying guests?

She couldn't understand why such an obvious solution hadn't occurred to her right away. Her grandfather would never have considered it, but he had had a pension that was sufficient for his needs, and they had had each other.

It was early evening—an October day like today, but mild in a week of Indian summer—and Felicity had run across the causeway and the beach and knocked on the door of one of the cottages.

Mrs Clemo had 'done' for Gull Rock House ever since the Captain's wife and daughter-in-law had been taken. She listened to Felicity's plans, and Felicity was almost dancing with enthusiasm. 'I can do the cooking,' Felicity was a first-class cook, Mrs Clemo saw no problem there, 'if you'd help with the cleaning, and maybe Jessie would come in now the twins are at school . . .'

That was just a year ago. They had opened at Easter, and guests who came promised to return. They hoped to build up on recommendations and advertising, and Felicity had never regretted turning her home into a guesthouse. If she hadn't she would have lost it. It was a tough struggle and perhaps something of an obsession with her. It could lose her Gordon, but if it did she wouldn't be breaking her heart like Deirdre because she wouldn't have the time.

They warmed and dried in front of the fire, Deirdre sipping a brandy, and then went up to the room Deirdre would be using. That hadn't changed much either from the room Deirdre remembered. The furniture was old-fashioned—a little rosewood Victorian dressing table with an oval mirror, a wardrobe and chest of drawers, and a bed with brass knobs and a white quilt. Faded roses covered carpet and wallpaper, and the grey skies outside couldn't dim the charm of the room.

Deirdre put her case on the floor, then sat on the bed and asked, 'Have you told Mrs Clemo why I'm here?'

'I said you felt like a holiday, that you were run down.'

'Oh, I'm so unhappy!' Without warning she covered her face with her hands and burst into floods of tears, and Felicity sat down beside her and put an arm around the shaking shoulders, making comforting sounds.

'I know I'm behaving like a fool,' Deirdre wept, 'but he was everything I wanted. He made himself my life. I thought we should always be together, and then it all finished. It was worse than somebody dying!'

Felicity knew how that felt, although part of her must have been prepared for the loss of her grandfather, who was an old man. To lose a young lover, with whom you had wanted to spend the rest of your life, would be a savage blow, and she said sympathetically, 'You've had a rotten deal, but take it from me, you are absolutely fantastic. There are bound to be other men——'

'There always have been,' Deirdre's voice was dull and hopeless and the tears in her eyes had no sparkle, 'but not like him.'

'You're sure it's all over?' Felicity wasn't exaggerating, Deirdre was so stunning that it was hard to imagine her being jilted, but she said,

'He won't see me. He won't answer my letters. Most of the time I can't get through to him on the phone, and when I do he cuts me off as soon as he can.'

It sounded like a classic case of terminal freeze, and Felicity thought, heaven protect me from laying myself open to that sort of treatment. Her pride wouldn't have worn it, but she could still pity Deirdre who had been badly treated and badly hurt. She needed to be taken around, taken out of herself. 'So how long can you stay?' she asked, and smiled. 'As a friend, of course— I'm not touting for custom. Although you might recommend us to anybody else who's coming this way!'

Deirdre wasn't smiling, her lips were still quivering with tears. 'Could—could I stay until I've sorted myself out?'

'As long as you like,' said Felicity warmly. This room was Deirdre's for as long as she needed it. It would be nice to have her here, she could move in for the winter if she wanted, and then the thought struck her, 'But what about your job?'

'I've given in my notice.'

Resigning was a drastic move these days, it had seemed a good job, well paid and interesting, but that was Deirdre's business and she never had been very practical. Felicity bit her lip and stayed silent, and Deirdre went on, 'I might go out to my mother, she's living in the South of France—I don't know.'

'That sounds nice,' said Felicity, and wondered if the years had made Deirdre's mother more loving.

'Nice!' Deirdre gave a short and bitter laugh. 'Except that she's only just admitting she's got a daughter. I don't know how she'd react to being turned into a grandmother.'

'You mean——?' Felicity gestured vaguely.

'Very likely,' said Deirdre.

'Oh dear! Oh, I am sorry.' That would complicate the future. 'Does he know?'

Deirdre shook her head. 'I wrote him another letter after you phoned me yesterday and asked him to get in touch. I gave him your address. I didn't tell him I thought I was pregnant, but I did say I was desperate.'

There was no phone in this house, and usually Mrs Clemo brought out the morning mail. Felicity wondered if Deirdre had used the word 'desperate' before. If she had been phoning and writing and depressed enough to consider suicide she probably had, and her final letter would be no more likely than the others to get the response she wanted.

He probably wouldn't even answer it, and Deirdre would wait and weep, unless Felicity could keep her occupied and entertained. There was a flourishing artists' colony along the coast, including some of Felicity's friends. She would take Deirdre along there tomorrow, otherwise Deirdre might be spending her time sitting on the rocks in the rain, sighing and looking out to sea.

That was a dreary prospect, and Felicity said brightly, 'We've a nice family in this week—parents and a couple of kids. They've gone to Truro for the day.'

Deirdre didn't seem to hear. She was opening her case and taking out a studio portrait of a man. She put it on the table by the bed so that when she turned her head on the pillow she could look straight at it, and Felicity found herself frowning because he seemed vaguely familiar.

The background was black. Light highlighted thick fair hair that flopped over his forehead. It was a strong face with a long mocking mouth, that could have been amused or cruel. Or both.

'What's his name?' Felicity asked.

Deirdre hadn't told her that. Now she said, 'David Holle,' looking at the photograph as though it might answer.

The name rang no bells with Felicity, but perhaps she had seen him some time. As the old saying had it, the world's a small place. 'Haven't I seen this photograph?' she mused. 'I feel as if I ought to know him. What does he do?'

'Writes,' said Deirdre. 'For television, mostly.' She named a couple of long-running series and Felicity nodded.

'That's where I must have seen this.' There was probably an article about him, although she couldn't remember it. She frowned. 'Do you think it's a good idea to put him where you'll see him last thing at night and first thing in the morning?'

'I see him all the time,' said Deirdre huskily. But she placed the photograph in the top drawer of the chest of drawers and picked up a little ornament that was made of pebbles, one beautiful pearl-pink shell, and a small gnarled piece of driftwood.

'I make them,' said Felicity. 'They're sort of sea sculptures, I call them sea-spells. They sell quite well, actually.'

'Pretty,' said Deirdre. She traced the lines of the shell with a fingertip. 'Do you remember that shell you had at school? How you used to sit and listen to that when things got grim?'

Every school holiday Felicity had brought back a shell from this beach.

'The sea-witch.' Deirdre was smiling now, although her cheeks were still streaked with tears. 'Can you work any magic for me?'

'Let's try, shall we?' Felicity's quick grin lit up her face. She didn't give much for the chances of a happy ending for Deirdre's love affair, but perhaps a holiday would work a little magic. She told Deirdre, 'You get unpacked. My living room now, and my bedroom, is what used to be my grandfather's room. With the big desk in—you remember?' Deirdre nodded. 'I'll be in there,' said Felicity.

As she left the room Deirdre said softly, 'We didn't even have a quarrel—I suppose he just got tired of me.'

That did make it sound hopeless. Felicity sighed, and decided that the mouth of the man in the photograph had been cruel.

She went into the only room with 'Private' on the door. Family portraits hung on the walls. Old navigation maps, pictures of ships, from sketches of full-masted schooners to a photograph of a wartime destroyer and the ocean-going cargo ship that had been her grandfather's last command.

In the window was a telescope and a huge Victorian globe of the world and a desk. The desk had a typewriter and was piled with business papers. There were chairs around a fireplace, a low table, a divan bed in an alcove and along one wall a wide shelf with some of the bits and pieces she had collected to make her 'sea-spells', and several models in the course of completion.

She sat down at the desk, elbows on the typewriter, head between clenched fists, and sighed again. She wasn't qualified for mending broken hearts. She was deeply sorry for Deirdre, but at a loss how to advise her. It seemed a mistake to give up her job, being unemployed wasn't going to make her feel less rejected, and if she was pregnant surely the man should be told. If she was going through with it. Felicity dreaded being asked what she thought Deirdre should do about that.

There was a photograph of Gordon on the desk. He had given it to Felicity a few months ago. It was a good likeness, showing a thin-faced young man, smiling enigmatically. It made him look mysterious, a deep thinker. She had wondered what her grandfather would have said about it, because he hadn't been over-impressed by Gordon. 'A personable enough young man, but not for you,' he had pronounced when Gordon started dating Felicity.

'And what makes you think I wouldn't settle for a personable fellow?' she had teased, and he had said,

'Because there's a wildness in you. One day you're going to call up the storm, and he's not the one to weather that.'

She had laughed then, although when she realised that her grandfather wasn't laughing she had stopped and said, 'I hope not! I don't like the sound of that at all.'

Now she sat with Gordon's photograph in front of her and thought, I won't get much encouragement from Gordon if I tell him I'm taking in old friends with broken hearts. He was always saying she had taken on too much with the guest-house, because it meant her free time was nil. He thought her own love life was a mess, and he was right, and more patient than she deserved.

When she took Deirdre along to meet her friends she would have to introduce Gordon to her, and she was so gorgeous that perhaps he would fall for her. Felicity wouldn't much care for that. But Deirdre wouldn't fall for him. Gordon wasn't going to blot out the memory of the man whose photograph Deirdre had just taken out of her case.

Felicity shouldn't be thinking that way, and she said,

'I love you,' to Gordon's picture, as she often said to Gordon, usually when he was complaining because she couldn't get away. 'Not as much as you love that house of yours,' he would moan, and she would say, 'It's my living as well as my home, but it's only a house. Of course I don't love it like I love you.'

Deirdre tapped on the door and opened it. She had changed into a mulberry-red crêpe dress that would look shapeless and dowdy on the hanger, but that moulded itself to her figure and was probably very expensive.

She came over to the desk and picked up the photograph. 'That's Gordon,' Felicity explained. 'I used to work in his galleries.' She had told Deirdre that on earlier Christmas cards. 'I've been going around with him for a long time.'

'Serious?' Deirdre squinted at the photograph and decided, 'He looks serious. And clever.'

'He is serious,' said Felicity. 'And so-so clever—you know, your Mr Average.'

'David's clever,' said Deirdre, putting Gordon's photograph back on the desk and turning away. 'He's brilliant. Do you think the baby will be clever? With David's brains and my looks. Although suppose it happens the other way? Well, that might not be so bad either. I'm not that dim and he's very good-looking.' Deirdre was pacing the room, her skirt swishing around her long slim legs. She stopped suddenly and her face crumpled. 'Oh, Felicity, what am I going to *do*?'

'About the baby?'

'About everything. I want him back so badly, but if he doesn't answer that last letter it's all over.' Her face was a mask of misery. 'And I know that he isn't going to answer it.'

Felicity's natural optimism surfaced, 'He might. But

if he doesn't I think you still ought to tell him about the baby. Whatever you decide.'

Deirdre looked slim as a reed, almost emaciated. It had to be early days. She was standing by the old globe, twirling it slowly around. She said, 'Do you mind if I talk about him?'

'Of course I don't mind.'

'I don't make friends easily. I'm not much better at it now than I was at school.' As Felicity started to protest she went on, 'They were your friends. They liked me because they liked you. David seemed different, he was very kind at first, he was the only man I really trusted, and now I know I've got to get over him and I haven't been able to talk much about it to anybody. But I could talk to you.'

'You do that,' said Felicity warmly.

'Don't tell anyone else, will you?' Deirdre shot her an apprehensive glance, and she promised,

'No. Although Mrs Clemo can be a comfort, I've cried on her shoulder more than once.'

'Because a man walked out on you?' asked Deirdre.

'That too.' One of Felicity's crushes, when she was eighteen, had emigrated and Mrs Clemo had been sympathetic, and tactful when Felicity's spirits quickly perked up again. But during Felicity's bereavements Mrs Clemo had been a tower of kindness and comfort. She would have nothing but pity for Deirdre, although she would disapprove of the recklessness that could leave a baby without a father.

'I'd rather you didn't say anything to anybody,' said Deirdre. 'I'll just wait, and see if a letter comes, and if I could talk to you about David that would help me.'

'Talk all you want,' said Felicity, and Deirdre took her at her word.

She certainly had a fixation on David Holle. She

didn't mix with the other guests. Felicity always did, if they showed signs of wanting her company. She would take coffee and share a drink with them in the big old lounge where a fire was always burning at this time of year. But after dinner, when she hardly ate a thing, Deirdre sat alone, looking pale and beautiful and miles away in her thoughts.

She did offer to help with the washing up. Felicity usually cleared from the evening meal alone, unless there was a great deal when Jessie, who worked as a waitress, would stay late, or some might get left until Jessie's mother arrived after breakfast.

With only four guests, and Deirdre, Felicity could manage. Deirdre seemed worn out and Felicity suggested, 'You go up to bed, you've had a long day.' But Deirdre lingered.

'Aren't you tired?' she asked. 'Doesn't it shatter you, running around after other people?'

'Sometimes, when we're full,' Felicity admitted. 'But that isn't too often, unfortunately, and the season's nearly over now. I do have some bookings for parties, though, there's one next week.'

'Why don't you buy a dishwasher?'

Felicity, in yellow rubber gloves, swished the suds in the deep sink and explained patiently, 'Because I can't afford one. I've had a lot of expenses. Next year maybe, if I'm showing a profit.'

'It sounds like awfully hard work.' Deirdre was concerned, then she remembered, 'But you always did have lots of energy, didn't you. You're lucky. I get so tired,' and she sat down on one of the kitchen chairs, her shoulders drooping. 'You're like David in that. He's got tremendous energy. He rides, swims, plays squash. And works, of course.'

'Sounds very restless,' said Felicity, stacking wet

plates in the rack on the sink to drain.

'No.' Deirdre was suddenly animated. 'No, that's something else about him. He never seems to hurry, and yet he gets more done than anybody else I've ever met.' Felicity turned to look at her and she was dreamy-eyed, with the yearning wistful look of a girl in love.

Oh *dear*! thought Felicity.

'He's very controlled.' Deirdre was smiling and speaking softly as though he was in the room. 'Very dominating.'

'Do you like being dominated?' Felicity hated it, but Deirdre went on smiling. 'I did with David, because he took such care of me.'

'Did he hell!' Felicity muttered, then bit her lip, 'Sorry,' but Deirdre was reliving memories.

'He'd have liked that dinner tonight.' The main course had been poached mackerel with gooseberry sauce—Felicity was specialising in Cornish cooking—followed by apple pie and Cornish cream; and Deirdre went on to describe meals that she and David had shared, from grand dinners in grand restaurants to cosy intimate twosomes.

Felicity nodded and murmured, 'Mmm, lovely,' and occasionally, 'What's that, then?' and got on with her work while Deirdre talked and talked. Not only menus but conversation—what he had said, what she had said. The affair had lasted six months, starting when her car broke down in a country lane and David Holle had stopped to help, growing and glowing and then, on his part, inexplicably cooling.

Felicity finished in the kitchen and went through to the dining room. The lounge was empty now, the guests had gone to bed, but Deirdre was still talking while Felicity laid a breakfast table. 'I gulp something down in the kitchen,' said Felicity, 'but if you like to eat in here that's fine, or I could bring you a tray up.'

'Just a black coffee any time,' said Deirdre. 'I'm not eating much these days, nor sleeping much either. But at least I won't be waiting for a phone to ring here, will I?'

'Tomorrow,' said Felicity, 'I'll take you along to meet some of my friends, but I warn you, most of them will want to paint you. There are a lot of artists along this coast and you'll be the best-looking gal they've seen for a long time.' She grinned. 'No fooling!'

'David paints,' said Deirdre.

'Walls or pictures?' said Felicity wearily.

'Pictures, of course.' Deirdre wasn't joking. 'He's very good.'

'Of course,' said Felicity.

'Matisse and Turner are his favourite artists. He's got a Turner.'

'That's nice for him.'

A watercolour, hanging on the wall, in the dining room, was a stormy sunset of sky and ocean, with blurring scarlet and purple, greens and black. It had hung here for the last fifty years, Deirdre must have seen it when she came here on school holidays, but now she examined it with fresh interest and asked, 'I suppose that isn't a Turner?'

'No such luck,' said Felicity. 'It's Josiah Tressilian who used to be a coastguard. He liked painting in the rain.'

'Oh,' said Deirdre, although Felicity had been fooling about the rain.

In the kitchen Sam was finishing his supper, skittering a heavy dish across the flagstones. He slept where he always slept, in Felicity's room that used to be her grandfather's. He was still the Captain's dog. In the night she heard his eager yelps as he ran in dreams along the sands beside his master; and sometimes he would listen, head cocked, eyes bright, then let his head fall with a despondency that always found an echo in Felicity.

'I dread the nights now,' Deirdre confided, as the two girls went upstairs with Sam padding like a black shadow behind. 'I brought my sleeping pills,' and Felicity stopped on the top step. After that letter the idea of Deirdre with a bottle of sleeping pills made her uneasy.

'I can make you a hot drink that will work a lot better,' she offered.

Deirdre thanked her and went on along the corridor. Sam stretched out in front of the door marked 'Private', and Felicity went down again to the kitchen to heat some milk, lace it liberally with whisky, add sugar and sprinkle with cinnamon. She would feel happier if she could persuade Deirdre to hand over the sleeping pills. You could wake with a thick head after half a tumbler of whisky, but you would wake.

She gave Deirdre time to wash and get into bed before she went back. Deirdre had the photograph out again and was sitting up huddled under the sheets, with the photograph on the side table. When Felicity walked in she explained huskily, 'I'm just saying goodnight.'

'Have you said it?' asked Felicity. He looked so sure of himself, and Deirdre looked so woeful, that the little tableau irritated her. 'Can I put him back in his drawer?'

'I suppose so,' said Deirdre.

'Goodnight, sweet prince,' Felicity muttered. Deirdre was carrying on as though he was a knight on a white charger, instead of a thoroughly selfish character who had taken far more than he had given. When Felicity opened the drawer she gasped, 'What are all these pills for?'

Deirdre shrugged, 'I get headaches.' There was a packet of non-prescription painkillers, but Felicity was more concerned about the other containers.

'And the rest——' she asked.

Deirdre shrugged, 'Some for day, some for night.'

Pep pills and sleeping pills. If Deirdre was taking the pills that were supposed to cheer her up they weren't doing a very good job, but it was the sleeping pills that scared Felicity. She picked up the Mogodons and said, 'I'd be a lot happier if you let me keep these in my room. If you need them you can have them, of course, but please let me keep them.'

'Well——' Deirdre hesitated, then said, 'all right.'

'Drink up,' said Felicity and Deirdre sipped and spluttered. 'That's the secret ingredient,' said Felicity gaily. 'A touch of the witch's brew.'

'It tastes like whisky.'

'Do you think so? Sleep well, it's going to be lovely having you here.'

'I'm so glad you sent me that card,' said Deirdre. 'And oh, I *wish* I was like you! Nothing ever got you down, I remember.'

Felicity went out of the room smiling, but the smile faded as soon as she closed the door behind her, and she pushed her hair back as though she was starting a headache herself. She didn't feel all that resilient tonight.

Sam had settled himself on his rug and Felicity kicked off her shoes and slowly began to undress. The rain had stopped. The only sound now was the waves breaking over the rocks. She loved that sound. She drew her strength from it. Most nights, no matter how weary she was, she relaxed as she shed her clothes, letting the cares of the day drop away.

But tonight she wasn't relaxing. When she got into her bathrobe her body was tense, her mind still racing. A warm bath might help. It would be crazy if Felicity couldn't sleep tonight, she was usually out like a light, the moment her head touched the pillow.

Deirdre's troubles were worrying her, of course, and the suspicion that she had invited two guests into her home when she invited Deirdre. The second a man whose name was already grating on her nerves.

'David Holle,' she said aloud, and her hands jerked out instinctively, fingers wide in a pushing gesture, as though someone dangerous was coming towards her and she had to hold him away.

CHAPTER TWO

DAWN was breaking when Felicity woke, regular as clockwork just before seven. Her room overlooked the open sea and the first thing she always did, when she got out of bed, was to go to the window and look out. Whether it was wet or fine she would open the window wider and take deep breaths of salt air, and it was better than a first cup of coffee to brighten her eyes and get the blood tingling in her veins. After a few moments of this she was usually almost ready to face the day.

This morning the skies were streaked with pearl, and there was no wind or rain lashing the sea, so, with luck, the weather had improved and she could take Deirdre out with her. And, perhaps, get her mind off David Holle for a while.

Nobody else was stirring, not even Sam, who grunted but declined to move. When Felicity reached Deirdre's door she opened it very quietly and listened to the rhythmic breathing coming from the bed. Then she went downstairs, to light the fire in the dining room, revive the fire in the lounge that was 'backed up' for the night, and start on the day's packed lunches. This was all routine. She did it fast and competently, planning her day in her mind.

By nine o'clock there was a glimmer of sunshine. The paying guests had left for Tintagel with their luncheon boxes, congratulating themselves that the weather had taken a turn for the better. Mrs Clemo arrived with the mail while Felicity was washing up after breakfast and announced, 'Better this morning. All by yourself?' looking around for Deirdre.

'She's not down yet,' said Felicity, peeling off her rubber gloves and pouncing on the three envelopes that Mrs Clemo had dropped on the kitchen table. They were all addressed to her, and although she hadn't expected anything for Deirdre she was disappointed.

'Waiting for something special?' enquired Mrs Clemo, who didn't miss much.

'Not really.' Felicity opened the two brown envelopes, one contained a bill, the other a receipt. Then the handwritten one, a letter from a man who had already made two stays this year.

Like several of her customers he had taken a fancy to Felicity. She was friendly with everyone who stayed. It was good for business and for happy holidays. This letter said that Edward Cunliffe might be down her way again soon, and if he was he would certainly be calling at Gull Rock House.

She handed it to Mrs Clemo. 'There's a man who appreciates my cooking!'

'And not only your cooking,' said Mrs Clemo.

He had seemed lonely, doing a walking tour on his

own, and Felicity had told him about places of interest and beauty spots within a ten-mile radius. He had only intended to stay overnight, but she made the area sound so beguiling that he was at Gull Rock House for over a week. He also seemed to find Felicity beguiling, which was probably why he had come back again and why he was writing to her now.

'She doesn't smile much, does she?' said Mrs Clemo, putting down the letter and returning to the subject of Deirdre. 'But she wasn't a cheerful child, as I recall. How long is she staying?'

'As long as she likes,' said Felicity. 'And she's a guest, not a customer.'

'Can you afford that?' Mrs Clemo knew that Felicity was operating on a shoestring, but Felicity said firmly,

'I've invited her, and it's a bad do if I can't ask a friend to stay. Besides——' She put toast in the toaster and tried to enlist Mrs Clemo's sympathies for Deirdre without betraying any confidences, 'Besides, she's—er—just lost her job and she's feeling depressed, and we're going to feed her up and cheer her up.'

'She's taking losing her job hard. Jessie said she hardly touched her dinner.'

'It was a shock,' said Felicity. 'That's how it often happens these days.'

Mrs Clemo knew all about that, and she asked no more questions. But her expression was puzzled as she watched Felicity putting toast and marmalade and coffee on a tray.

Deirdre opened her eyes when Felicity walked into the bedroom. 'Not too bad a day today,' said Felicity.

'Has the post come?'

'There isn't anything, but even if he wrote right away I doubt if it would have arrived yet.' And if he did write there was no guarantee that he would say, 'I love you. I miss you.' It could easily be a goodbye letter sent here where Deirdre couldn't reach him in a hurry.

'Come down as soon as you're ready,' said Felicity.

They set off as soon as Deirdre was ready, leaving Mrs Clemo in charge. First stop was a market, to buy fresh vegetables, where Felicity, who always dealt with the same farming family, was greeted as a friend and served with the bargains.

She introduced Deirdre over the cauliflowers, and Deirdre smiled and moved away to a pottery stall, picking up mugs and reading the inscriptions until Felicity joined her. 'Sorry about this,' said Felicity, carrying two large well-filled bags, 'but the food has to come first, and this is where I can buy the cheapest and the best. I'll put it in the car and then we'll look round the rest of the market.'

'Would you mind if we didn't?' Deirdre hunched her shoulders as if a cold wind was blowing, although it was quite mild today. 'Only the last time I went through a market——'

She was with David Holle, presumably. 'Of course I don't mind,' said Felicity. 'We'll get on, then.'

In the car as they drove along the coast road Deirdre reminisced about how David had bought her a tortoiseshell-backed mirror from Petticoat Lane one weekend when she felt she had been upstaged at work. 'He said, "Any time anyone tells you you're less than the best take a look in here".'

'A silver tongue too,' said Felicity a little tartly. 'Mind you, he was right. If I had your face I'd enjoy looking in mirrors.'

'My face didn't stop him getting tired of me,' said Deirdre sadly.

Felicity began to tell her about the artists they were on their way to meet, sculptors, and painters, living in

Fenmouth where Felicity had once worked. On the
outskirts of town was a cobbled courtyard, and a little
artists' colony. Felicity dropped in fairly regularly,
short visits because she was usually rushed off her feet,
but keeping in touch with friends.

She realised quite soon that Deirdre wasn't listening.
There were some riotous characters among them, and
some quite well-known names, but Deirdre sat blank-
faced, showing no reaction and no interest.

Felicity was describing a painting that one artist had
shown in this year's Royal Academy exhibition. She
went on, in the same conversational tones, 'He also
changes into a werewolf at the full moon. That's a well-
known fact.'

At that Deirdre turned, a faint frown-line between
her brows. 'What?'

'You'll like him,' said Felicity.

'Will I?' Deirdre either decided she had misheard or
even werewolves weren't getting through to her, so
Felicity shut up and they did the rest of the short trip in
silence.

'Down that alley,' Felicity pointed it out as they
passed. 'I can usually manage to park just around the
corner,' and Deirdre sat up.

'Can I stay in the car? I'm sorry, but I'd rather not
meet anybody. I don't want to keep you from your
friends, but I want to be on my own. Well, I don't mind
being with you, but not other people, not just yet.'

Perhaps Felicity was being insensitive. Deirdre had
said this was like a bereavement and it might be
unfeeling to force her to meet strangers, who would
want to know all about her and could intrude on her
grief. Perhaps it wasn't cheering up she needed so much
as quiet support.

Felicity went on driving. 'You don't have to meet a

soul if you don't want to. I have to call in at the Galleries because I've got some work to deliver, and if you'd like to take a look at Gordon come in with me. Or you can stay in the car, I won't be more than a few minutes.'

Deirdre decided not to see Gordon either, and Felicity left her in the car park behind the shop listening to a cassette playing love songs.

Felicity's work had a small corner display all to itself in here, and a notice, 'Sea-Spells by Felicity Mayne.' That was favouritism, in other shops they took their chance among other goods, but they were quite popular and she could rely on getting rid of most of them sooner or later.

She had a dozen new designs with her, carefully packed in tissue paper in a cardboard box, and she was expected and the staff knew her. 'He's in the office,' said the woman who spotted her first, and Felicity said, 'Thanks,' and tapped on the door.

'Come!' called Gordon. He was behind a desk going through a sheaf of accounts and his face brightened when he looked up and saw Felicity. He was a slim good-looking young man, rather diffident, almost shy at times, and Felicity's energy and zest had fascinated him from the first day she came to work here. He wished she had never left. 'Hello, stranger,' he said.

'Ah, don't be like that!' She pulled a pleading face. 'I saw you on Sunday night.'

He corrected her, '*I* saw *you* on Sunday night.' He had been the one who came out to her home, as he usually was, and it was no use telling him how hard it was for her to get away, because he knew that, but he still resented it.

She couldn't even stay for lunch now. When she said,

'I've got someone in the car, I said I'd take her straight back,' he asked,

'One of your paying guests?'

'Well, yes.' If she explained that it was an old school friend he would expect to be introduced.

'You've started running a taxi service for them?'

'It's an idea.' She smiled, and so did he, reluctantly.

'I would be the fool to put that into your head.'

They were both joking, and she showed him the new models and he nodded approval. Nobody ever claimed they were art, but they were attractive inexpensive gifts and mementoes for the holidaymakers to take back home. The money they made helped to keep the guest-house solvent.

When the box was unpacked and Felicity had her cheque from last month's consignment she said, 'I'll have to go,' and lifted her face to be kissed. She wished she hadn't brought Deirdre and could have allowed herself an hour or so with Gordon, because she was very fond of him. He was kind, he always had been. She always felt happy in his arms, and although this kiss was brief it was tender. He could hardly kiss her passionately when the office door might open any moment. Gordon wasn't the sort to lose his head and make a fool of himself. Come to that, he was not a passionate man. There would be no mad ecstasy with Gordon to blow a girl's mind and leave her open to the kind of hurt that Deirdre was enduring.

'I'll see you to the car,' he said, but the phone rang and as he answered Felicity gave a little wave and mouthed, ' 'Bye, love.'

Deirdre hadn't moved. She was still hunched, her expression still one of deep sadness, and again Felicity thanked her stars for Gordon. She really should start appreciating him more.

'You're back early,' said Mrs Clemo when they walked into the house.

'I had a headache,' said Deirdre. She was so pale and drawn these days that she looked as if it was true. She said, 'Sorry to be a killjoy,' and Felicity said breezily,

'Oh, I can use the time here, believe me. I'll do some modelling. Tell you what, we'll take some soup up and you can rest and we can natter while I work.'

The 'natter' consisted, as she had known it would, of a monologue by Deirdre, and Felicity realised that she was going to get the whole six months of the affair in detail. Days, and very probably nights.

Well, that was how psychiatrists operated. They let their patients talk it out, act it out. Listening was the least she could do for an old friend . . .

No letters came. After that first morning Deirdre was usually downstairs before Mrs Clemo arrived, and when there was no mail for her she would turn away. Felicity tried to pretend, 'She's applied for another job, she's waiting to hear.'

'Must have set her heart on it,' said Mrs Clemo, with more than a trace of scepticism, and Felicity was sure that both Mrs Clemo and Jessie suspected what the real trouble was.

Deirdre was suffering, and Felicity shared her pain, because whenever the girls were alone Deirdre went on with the saga of David Holle. She seemed to have photographic memories and she shared them, walking along the beach gathering materials for Felicity's models, at night while Felicity was clearing up. Felicity tried hard to interest her in something, anything else, but she didn't want to meet other people, and it was hard work to coax even a smile from her.

She tried several times to phone David from the boathouse, and got no reply, and that hadn't helped.

Neither did the weather. All week storms had built up along the coastline, but one thing Felicity was determined about, Deirdre was staying downstairs for the party that was being held at Gull Rock House ten days after she arrived. She *needed* new faces. The guests were mostly Felicity's artist friends, and Deirdre would look beautiful, and perhaps she would stop thinking about the past for a while, if the present was bright and cheerful and friendly.

'I could do with some help,' Felicity said. 'It's a buffet meal, and if you could give us a hand with the drinks.'

'Of course,' said Deirdre without much enthusiasm.

Party day kept Felicity on the run from early morning. During the winter months when nobody came here on holiday, catering for the occasional party could be a godsend and she was giving them value for money. The food had to be just right, a picture to look at and delicious to eat. She had put a great deal of thought and trouble into the buffet and set it out in the dining area, an attractive room with low ceiling and white walls, overlooking the sea.

Deirdre helped Felicity and Jessie and Mrs Clemo carry the dishes from the kitchen, move furniture around and make everything ready, but just before the guests were due she went up to her room.

Felicity thought she was changing, and when cars began arriving on the quayside, people spilling out, ran upstairs to hurry her up. Deirdre was still in jeans and jumper, sitting in front of the electric fire in her bedroom with a bottle beside her and a glass of white wine.

As Felicity opened the door she begged, 'Don't scold me, I'll try to come down. But it is an engagement party, isn't it?' Any other party, except a wedding reception, would have been preferable, but this was what it was, and Felicity couldn't hang around. She had to be waiting to welcome them. 'I'll give you half an hour,' she said, 'then I'm coming back to fetch you, and I'm taking no excuses.' She nodded towards the bottle. 'Have another glass and get into the party mood.'

It was well over an hour before she could slip away again and by then Deirdre had had several more glasses of wine, but they hadn't produced the party spirit. She had the photograph out and her eyes were puffed, and Felicity swore softly.

Deirdre was not joining the company tonight. 'I'm s-sorry,' she said, and Felicity resisted an impulse to snatch David Holle's photograph out of her hands and hurl it through the window. How could a man do this to a girl? What I'd like to say to him! she thought. To Deirdre she said, 'All right, you've made your point, you're not coming down.'

At least the party was a success. It went on until the early hours, and it wasn't until everyone had gone, and Felicity looked around at the clearing up that had to be done, that she realised how worn out she was.

Mrs Clemo and Jessie would be over early in the morning, but she couldn't leave all this, and she began to stack plates on to the trolley. When Deirdre walked into the dining room she said, with a tired grin, 'You missed 'em.'

'I know.' Well, of course she knew. Felicity had been trying to joke.

'Was it a success?' Deirdre went to the window, looking out over the dark sea into the dark night. 'Were they happy?'

'Everyone was very happy.' Felicity's eyes were blurring, and her feet were aching. She had been in the kitchen for hours preparing all the food, and on her feet since seven o'clock last night looking after the guests.

Deirdre opened a door that led to a little landing stage at the back of the house, where a dinghy was moored during the summer months, and Felicity felt the rush of cold air.

It was stuffy in here with a haze of cigarette smoke. She could use some fresh air herself and she wondered if Deirdre was up to helping with the washing up. 'Oh, I miss him so!' Deirdre's mournful voice drifted in, and Felicity could take no more of that tonight.

'You can't lock yourself away from the world,' she said, to the open door and the girl beyond it.

'There's nothing left in my world,' Deirdre sighed.

'Of *course* there is!' She could start by helping to shift some of this.

'Nothing.'

Felicity rolled her eyes heavenwards. She mustn't snap at Deirdre. Right now she had better persuade her to go back to bed, she would be more nuisance than use down here.

Over the sound of the sea came the sound of a splash, and Felicity dropped a couple of glass dishes with a strangled 'Oh, *no!*' She couldn't believe it. She ran, kicking off her shoes, but she couldn't believe her eyes even when the little landing stage was empty and she could see Deirdre in the churning water below, the currents already carrying her away from the lights of the house. There was no moon and she had never been a strong swimmer.

'*No!*' Felicity shrieked again, the moment before she herself hit the water. It was paralysingly cold, but she swam fast clutching Deirdre's floating hair, gripping her shoulders and back, kicking, heading for the landing stage where she half dragged, half carried Deirdre, choking and spluttering, up the steps, into the house.

As soon as she loosed her hold Deirdre collapsed in a shivering heap.

The fire in the lounge was still burning, this room was chilled from the open door. 'Come on!' Felicity had her on her feet again, stumbling along. 'We've got to get out of these clothes.' It had all happened so quickly that her mind was whirling, but suddenly the confusion crystallised into anger and she turned fiercely, eyes blazing, 'You *stupid* cow, did you do that on purpose?'

Great retching sobs were Deirdre's only answer, and Felicity left her in front of the fire and raced to fetch towels, and turn on the hot tap in the bath. She stripped off her own dress and undies in the bathroom and hurried back barefoot, wearing a towelling robe, her wet hair dripping down her neck and face.

Deirdre hadn't moved and Felicity, shocked and shaken, snapped, 'If your mind's set on it, sit there and get your death of cold.'

'It was an accident,' said Deirdre huskily, then, 'I think,' and Felicity's anger subsided. Deirdre must still be terribly unhappy, and Felicity knelt down and eased off one sodden shoe, the other had vanished. 'I could have drowned,' said Deirdre shakily. 'We both could.'

'Yes,' Felicity had to agree, but she wasn't feeling too proud of herself because Deirdre's stay down here had done nothing towards healing her heartbreak. 'I'm running you a hot bath,' she said.

Deirdre went obediently to the bathroom and got into the bath, while Felicity washed her own hair in the handbasin, at a loss for words. Scolding was worse than useless, but tomorrow there would have to be talk, because Deirdre *could* have drowned. Felicity swam like a fish, but she could have walked out of that room and not heard the splash. Deirdre was still at appalling risk unless something like a miracle happened.

'I'm not pregnant,' said Deirdre suddenly. She lay full length in the steaming water, her hair floating, her face an unaccustomed pink from the heat of the bath. 'That was wishful thinking, I made a mistake about that too. That made me feel even more miserable, but it does mean that I can make a fresh start, doesn't it?'

'Of course you can.' Felicity raised her own dripping head, hope springing at the words 'fresh start'.

'How long was I in the water before you reached me?'

'Hardly any time.' Felicity began to towel her hair, starting to smile because Deirdre was sounding different as she sat up and said,

'Long enough to think I was drowning.' A few seconds in the black choking sea would be long enough for that. Her voice was getting stronger, charged with wonder. 'You know, I feel as if part of my life ended and this is a new beginning. As if I've been given a second chance.' She took a deep breath. 'I don't need——' Another breath and this time she said it loud and clear, 'I don't need David any more.'

Felicity gave a whoop of glee, 'Now that is talking sense!'

Deirdre got out of the bath and briskly towelled herself dry, deciding, 'I shall go out to my mother. I shall get some sunshine and miss the winter.'

'That's a great idea,' Felicity applauded.

'And if a letter should come here—he's the only one I've given this address—tear it up, because I never want to hear his name again.'

'Me neither,' said Felicity fervently, and thought, I could write a book on the man. I feel as if I've been locked up with him for years in a very little room, and now I'm being let out and all I want to do is forget him . . .

Nearly drowning was a drastic cure for love, but it seemed to work, because next morning Deirdre sent a cable and booked a flight, and during the remaining three days of her stay at Tregorran Cove she never mentioned David Holle again.

When she said goodbye she thanked Felicity for letting her stay here and for saving her life. Whether she meant from the sea or from the half-life of deep depression Felicity wasn't sure, but it was a relief to kiss Deirdre goodbye and wave her on her way.

This insight into the cruelty of a heartless lover had been a searing experience for Felicity too, and she was glad it was over. Deirdre was flying into the sunshine and David Holle's shadow was lifted from Felicity.

'Good evening, is Miss Osborne still staying here?' he said, and Felicity felt as if she had opened her door and found herself facing a gun held in a steady hand. Dusk was falling fast. Mrs Clemo had gone home and Jessie hadn't come because there were no guests at the moment. Felicity had been upstairs when she heard the doorbell and she had hurried down, expecting Gordon maybe, or friends, or customers. Anybody but this man who was standing in the shadows on her doorstep.

He was exactly as Deirdre had described him—tall, broad-shouldered, thick fair hair that the wind had ruffled. The smile was the smile on the photograph and numbing shock held her so that it seemed to her she stood there speechless for ages.

She didn't. It was only a moment. She wanted to close the door on him, but she could hardly do that. She opened it a little wider and he stepped in, and she said, 'She left on Friday,' This was the following Tuesday. 'She'll be in the South of France by now. She was flying out to stay with her mother.'

His expression told nothing beyond casual interest. It wasn't even rueful, and yet he had come here to find

Deirdre. I'm glad she missed you, thought Felicity. She's better off without you.

'Can you put me up for the night?' he was asking, and this was a guest-house, you weren't supposed to turn people away. She wanted to say, 'Get out', but there were other things she wanted to say to him too, and if he had his luggage upstairs and was settled in he would be more likely to listen.

'Yes,' she said.

'Is the car all right on the quayside?' A flash job, the new Rover. She knew what car he had and he wouldn't want to leave that out in the open, unattended. 'Go through the archway,' she said. 'We park in the boatyard, it'll be all right there.'

She stood at the door and watched him striding over the stones of the causeway. She would feed him, she knew his tastes in food and wine and practically everything, and then she would tell him that he had almost driven Deirdre to her death. He should be told that. Deirdre was cured of him now, but if the currents had got her that night he would have been as responsible as if he had thrown her into the sea.

She went upstairs and opened a bedroom. Not the one Deirdre had had. He wasn't the sort you would put in a room with rosebuds on the wall, and later she would give him his photograph.

'Get rid of this for me,' Deirdre had said when she was packing, as though it was rubbish.

It was still in the chest of drawers. Felicity had intended to put it out with the rubbish later in the week. It was a pity that all the memories of David Holle couldn't be discarded so easily. Being told that he had behaved abominably wasn't going to worry a man like him. As far as he was concerned the heartbreak was Deirdre's hard luck, but hearing that she had tried to drown herself might sometimes prey on his mind in the dark of the night.

Felicity reached the top of the stairs as he opened the door, and came back into the house carrying a large holdall. The numbness that had paralysed her when she first saw him had gone now, and her senses and instincts seemed sharpened, like a wild animal in peril, warning her to be quiet and careful. She heard herself say, 'I'll show you your room.'

'Thank you.' He came up the stairs towards her, and she thought, I know that you have a scar on your left shoulder. I know how it came there.

She went ahead when he reached her. He would mention Deirdre soon. Let him start. She would say nothing until he did. Unless he never did, then she would bring down the photograph. She walked towards the room she had prepared for him, very conscious of him following behind her, feeling the weight of his shadow on her again.

The door of her room was open and Sam ambled out to investigate, blocking David Holle's way. Felicity said jerkily, 'He always comes out for big men. He hopes they're going to be my grandfather.' His eyes questioned her and she explained, 'He's a one-man dog and the man died.'

He stopped to scratch the smooth black head. Deirdre had told her he had once had a great black mongrel called Bruno. She wondered if there had been any retriever in Bruno, because David Holle was greeting Sam like an old friend, and Sam was displaying more animation than he had shown in a long time.

They were in the doorway of her room and through the open door David Holle saw the old maps on the walls and asked, 'May I?'

She didn't want him prying in there, but he had taken

her permission for granted and he was examining the maps. Then he turned and looked around. When her grandfather slept in here there had been no photographs, but when Felicity moved in, opening the rest of the house to the public, she had gone through old albums so that now she had a portrait gallery around her while she worked and slept. In their day they had all lived in this house, and their blood ran in her veins, and they made her feel less alone.

David Holle crossed to a misty study of a young woman in early Victorian dress, with wide tiptilted eyes, and remarked, 'She looks like you.'

'Does she?' She wasn't telling him who that was. She wasn't telling him anything, except about Deirdre when the time was right. She followed his glance to the desk in the window and thought, he's thinking he could work in here, and said quickly, 'This is my room. If you'll come along I'll show you yours.'

When she left him she went back and sat down at her desk and gripped her fingers together so that the knuckles gleamed white. He was a cool customer, but she had some news that should shake him. 'She tried to *drown* herself. And she nearly succeeded, damn you!' She glared at Gordon's thoughtful photograph then smiled, 'Not you, love. You never hurt a soul, did you? Not like the one whose bed I've just made up for the night.'

She was beginning to wish that she hadn't let him in, and it wasn't too late to say, 'I've changed my mind,' and tell him why, but ranting and raging would sound ridiculous. He had treated Deirdre badly, and she would be cool and cutting when she said so. In the meantime she would be civil and wary and bide her time.

She gave him the register to sign and she looked at

the entry as though it was news to her. 'London? Have you come down today?'

'I've been staying in Padstow,' he said, and that *was* news. The one thing Deirdre had not mentioned, and probably her main reason for coming down here, because Tregorran Cove was only about an hour's run from Padstow. She had been following him hoping he would follow her. But it had taken him nearly three weeks to make up his mind, and by then she had taken flight.

'Pretty place, Padstow,' said Felicity, and handed him the menu for the evening meal.

While she was in the kitchen preparing it Jessie arrived with a twin in tow. The car had been spotted, would Felicity be needing help? 'There's only the one,' said Felicity. 'For one night. I can handle him.'

Jessie knew nothing about David Holle. She and her mother had decided Miss Osborne had been let down by some man, but Felicity had kept Deirdre's confidence. She would have told Jessie now, but Kevin, aged ten, was not known as the nosiest kid for miles for nothing. He wouldn't have missed a word. In the morning Felicity would probably tell both her helpers the full story, but tonight she was on her own.

She produced a good meal because she always did. It would have bothered her more than him if the flavour of the lobster bisque had had less than perfect piquancy or the steak au poivre had been overdone, and when she produced the cheese board he said, 'That was excellent. I'd like to stay on for a couple of days.'

She had served him quickly, exchanging a few words between each course but not stopping to talk. Although each time she got back into the kitchen her hands were shaking.

Not after we've had our little talk, she thought.

You'll be away early after that. 'Guests are always welcome,' she said. 'Will you have your coffee in the lounge?'

'Will you join me?'

She intended to. She took in the tray a few minutes later and was a little taken aback at seeing him seated in the wooden armchair. Sam was on the rug in front of the fire, and David Holle sat easily in the chair, long legs crossed. Felicity stood holding her tray, frowning slightly. 'Wouldn't you find one of the padded ones more comfortable?'

'But they're not.'

So she had heard her grandfather say. She shrugged and put the coffee on a table. He asked for a brandy and asked her to join him in that too, and because she needed one she poured two good measures. She wasn't going to enjoy this. It had been stupid setting up the whole thing like a film set, when all she wanted to do was tell him how much she despised him.

'Black, please,' he said, 'One sugar,' and she had nearly handed him that before he spoke. 'How long have you been running this place?' he enquired.

She took a gulp of her brandy before she poured her own coffee. 'This is my first season.'

'Was it a going concern when you took it or are you starting from scratch?'

Deirdre couldn't have told him much about her, although why should she, a school friend she hadn't seen for years?

Felicity sat on the edge of a chair, balanced forward so that if she did have to get up quickly she could be out of the room fast. She wasn't anticipating violence, but she was about to accuse him of being a brute, and let loose anger and condemnation.

'It was my home,' she explained. 'I lived here with my

grandfather. If it works out I can afford to go on living here.'

'What's your name?' Didn't he even know that?

'Felicity Mayne.' He smiled, and she said quietly, 'It was a pity you missed her.'

'Miss Osborne. Yes.'

Her mind clicked. He was still referring to Deirdre as Miss Osborne, although he knew by now that he was talking to Felicity. So he wasn't aware that the two girls were old friends, and he could have no idea how Deirdre had talked, how much she had told Felicity. Felicity had all this encyclopaedic information about him, while he believed that he and she were strangers. It was like being a mind-reader.

And she knew that he was attracted to her. She knew the signs of that, and he wasn't hiding them. He was looking at her with frank admiration, and she thought, I could lead him on, I might even make him suffer a little.

She smiled slowly, her slanting sea-green' eyes glinting. I could get under his skin she thought, on a rising tide of excitement. If I wanted to I could get him.

CHAPTER THREE

FELICITY'S first thought next morning was of David Holle, and it jerked her up in bed like cold water on her face. Last night it had seemed a good idea to teach him a lesson. She couldn't hurt him as he had hurt Deirdre, but already she had made him want her and believe he was going to get her. Last night he thought he had met a girl uncannily on his wavelength, and if she had been meeting him for the first time, and Deirdre had told her nothing about him, she would have been impressed herself, because he was an exhilarating dominant personality, very much a man, not a boy.

She could understand how Deirdre had gone overboard for all that sexy strength. Deirdre, who lacked strength herself and who believed he was truly caring. He had turned up here at last, asking after her, but the speed at which he'd diverted his attention to Felicity showed that he was a womaniser. He deserved a little pain for the pain he caused, although in the cold morning light Felicity could see snags in her scheme.

Like him mentioning Deirdre to Jessie or Mrs Clemo. If they told him that Felicity and Deirdre had been at school together he'd know then that Deirdre would have discussed him with Felicity. Deirdre's name hadn't come up again last night, while they were sitting downstairs in the lounge, but if it did she would have to admit to the old days.

Last night they had talked about his work. Thanks to Deirdre she knew the titles of his TV plays and series, and she said as she sipped her brandy, 'Are you by any chance *the* David Holle?'

'That depends what you're associating me with.'

'The writer. The scriptwriter.'

He smiled, 'I didn't know that anyone read the credits.'

'I look out for yours. I'm one of your fans.' Of course she wasn't a fan, but she had seen some of his work and she had to admit that he was good.

Another snag was how Felicity would react when he wanted to make love to her, because physical attraction was the heart of the matter. There was a sexual buzz between them, based on antagonism on her part and lust on his. She wanted to lead him on enough to get him crazy for her, so she must be prepared for some contact and not snarl 'Keep your hands off me!' the moment he touched her.

She was at the window by now, doing her early morning deep breathing, and she looked down into the water and remembered Deirdre down there. I'll draw a little blood before I send him on his way, she promised herself, and turned so quickly that her elbow knocked one of her little sea-spells spinning off the window ledge. One fragile shell shattered against the desk, and she muttered 'Damn,' and stooped to scoop up the fragments, then swore again, louder, as a jagged edge pricked her fingertip. That was sharp, that hurt; and she watched a drop of blood well out and thought ruefully that it was ironic that the first blood spilt should be her own.

He had asked for breakfast at eight-thirty, coffee at eight, and she tapped on his door and when he called, 'Thank you,' put down the tray outside.

Sam was still sleeping. Felicity opened her own door and then left it ajar and said, as she often did, 'Come down when you feel like it,' and he came down half an hour later with David Holle. That was probably coincidence, but it riled her, seeing the man and the dog together, although she smiled and said, 'Good morning—don't let that dog bother you.'

'I won't.' Of course he wouldn't. He didn't let anybody bother him. He took his own time answering Deirdre's cry from the heart. But I'll bother you, Felicity vowed, and knew that she did already because she could feel the pull between them. The staircase came down into the lounge. She was near the bottom of the stairs and she moved away, heading for the dining room and the kitchen as he came towards her, because she believed that if she had stood her ground and he had reached her he would have caught her hand or touched her face.

In the dining room he took his table of the night before and she handed him the menu. No other tables were laid, and last night an individual lamp had burned on his. This morning daylight lit the room, and he looked across at Josiah Tressilian's watercolour, and Felicity said, 'I always think it looks a bit like Turner. If I ever strike it rich I'm going to buy myself a genuine Turner.'

The empty room didn't hold out much hope of her getting rich in a hurry, and if she ever did there were a good many things she would rather spend her money on, but he looked surprised.

'Funny you should say that. I have a Turner I'm very fond of.'

'You do?' She affected astonishment. 'Really? Well, I certainly envy you.'

'I must show it to you.' She could see it in her mind's eye, because Deirdre had described the picture and the place where it hung, over an Adam fireplace in his London flat.

'I'd like that,' she said. 'Do you do any painting yourself?'

'Only for my own amusement.'

'Like my sea-spells.' He waited for her to explain and she indicated one on a window ledge. 'I beachcomb for my materials and make them up for the visitors. I suppose——' she hesitated, then laughed. 'No, I'm not trying to sell you one, I shouldn't think they're your kind of thing. What I was going to say was that if you have no plans for this morning you might like to stroll along the beach after breakfast.'

He might have plans, although staying on here seemed to have been a spur-of-the-minute decision, but he said without hesitating, 'I think that's a very good idea.'

'Lovely,' she said, and gave him her widest smile.

While he ate breakfast she went upstairs to make his bed. Mrs Clemo would have done this, but Felicity needed to keep occupied. If she stopped to consider what she was doing she would have to admit that it was crazy. What right had she to be punishing David Holle for jilting Deirdre? Except that she had seen what it did to Deirdre, and she had pulled Deirdre out of the sea. It could be a dangerous game too, he might be a dangerous man when he found she was stringing him along. But if she was honest that was what made it so irresistible. The excitement. Getting the guest-house started, and trying to make it pay, was hard unremitting grind. She needed something to give a sharp edge to life. This could beat Russian roulette.

Having made the bed, and changed the towels, she picked up a jacket that was tossed over a chair, to hang it in the wardrobe, and a letter fell out. The Padstow address was in Deirdre's handwriting. The London postmark was the day she came here, and Felicity felt like a spy who has stumbled on a Top Secret document. After all, Deirdre's confidences reading this could hardly matter, but it would tell Felicity what David Holle knew about Gull Rock Guest-House.

This address was at the top and Deirdre had written, 'I'm just leaving for a holiday here, I don't know how long for, but please write to me. I keep saying that and getting no answer, but please, if it's only a line, oh, *please*, David! Or come. It isn't far from Padstow and I miss you so desperately. You must know how much, and you must know that I shall miss you and love you for eternity, D.'

Not quite for eternity, thanks to the shock of nearly

getting herself drowned, but when Deirdre wrote that she had been in despair, and a lot he had cared. She hadn't written again, Felicity was sure of that, so he didn't know why she had chosen this house. She slipped the letter back into the envelope and was then faced with the problem—which pocket? It seemed safer to leave the jacket where it was on the chair, with the letter beneath as though it had slipped out when he'd dropped the coat down.

She went downstairs again and busied herself in the kitchen until Mrs Clemo arrived. Mrs Clemo and David Holle had passed on the causeway, he on his way to get himself a newspaper, she coming here to do a few hours' housework. She was still looking impressed when she walked into the kitchen. 'Nice young man,' she remarked.

'You think so?'

'Very well set up. Only staying the night,' Jessie said.

'That was what he said when he came.'

'Has he changed his mind?' Mrs Clemo had brought the post as usual, including Felicity's bank statement, which was not actually in the red but low enough when Felicity thought of her own commitments. 'Yes,' she said vaguely, scanning figures, 'he could be here for another day or two.'

'Plenty of room,' said Mrs Clemo, an unnecessary comment as there were no other guests. 'Sam seems to have taken to him.'

Sam had gone with him. He had whistled and Sam had ambled off at his heels, and Felicity had had to bite her lip to stop herself calling the dog back. She supposed she ought to start telling Mrs Clemo about Deirdre. She should be saying, 'You never did believe that tale about her being made redundant and waiting to hear about another job, did you? You knew it was all over a man. Well, he turned up last night. Five days late or quite early enough, according to the way you look at it, because he gave her a hard time, and he would have done again if things had started up again, because as soon as he heard she wasn't here he settled for me. He's after me now, Mrs Clemo, and he thinks he's getting me. He isn't, of course, I think he's a swine, but I've decided to show him how it feels to want what he can't have. I'm going to lead him on and then give him his marching orders.'

'You're not, you know,' Mrs Clemo would have replied pretty briskly to that announcement, and she would have put every possible spoke in the wheel. So I'll tell them tomorrow, Felicity decided. I'll play today out first. 'He writes,' she said. 'For television mostly. His name's David Holle and he's just gone for a newspaper. When he comes back we're going for a walk along the beach.'

'Married man, is he?'

'This is a guest-house, not a marriage bureau. We don't usually ask them that—it's none of our business. Why are you asking that?'

'Because you've got a funny look about you,' said Mrs Clemo, taking off her brown woolly hat and hanging it with her brown tweed coat behind the kitchen door.

'Funny? What do you mean, funny?' queried Felicity.

'Just be careful, that's all.'

'I don't know what you mean.'

There had always been something in Felicity that set her apart. She was kind, gentle, loving, but there was what her grandfather called the wild streak. Mrs Clemo sighed and shook her head, admitting, 'I'm not so sure I know myself.'

But Felicity could see what Mrs Clemo had meant

when she'd described David Holle as 'well set up'. Just walking beside him, out of the house, Felicity was very conscious of the lithe co-ordination of his body, as well as the fact that he was taller than her by a head and shoulders. You could scramble down to the beach from the causeway, and when she took the first step he held out a hand and she laughed, 'I've been doing this all my life, I should be helping you down. Shout if you're slipping and I'll catch you.'

'That's the best offer I've had today,' he said, and they went down over the rocks, smiling at each other. I wish I hadn't brought him, she thought, because I'm going to stop smiling in a minute and tell him to get lost.

It was a cold day, with a pewter-dark sky and an angry sea, but she always enjoyed walking along the beach, picking up her bits and pieces, and she had been mad to spoil it for herself like this. The last time she had come collecting Deirdre had been with her, talking interminably about David Holle.

They walked now at the sea's edge and Felicity picked up shells: limpet, whelk, periwinkle. He was looking across at the house, seeing it from a new angle, remarking, 'I hadn't realised you backed right over the sea like that.'

'We're safe enough. The house was built for storms, rock on rock.' She selected half a dozen pebbles and placed them in her basket. 'But it's deep water at the back,' she said. 'Deep enough to drown.' She met his eyes and almost told him, 'Deirdre tried it.'

'Is this how it's always been? On the edge of the rocks?'

'For the last two hundred years or so. There were other houses once, long ago, farther out, and a church.' The rising wind blew her hair over her face and she tucked it behind her ears. 'On stormy nights you can sometimes hear the bells under the water.'

'You can?'

It was only a legend, but she went on with the story. 'We're nothing compared to Penhale Sands. Once Penhale was the ancient town of Langarroc. Came the night of the great storm and they vanished, but no less than *seven* peals of bells can be heard there.'

'And you've heard them?'

As a child she had always believed she heard the bells. She knew now that it was a child's imagination, but she smiled at the memory and said, 'You wouldn't believe me if I said I had.'

Sam had come with them. He wanted a stick thrown and had finally found a suitable one which he laid at David's feet. David threw it, without following its flight—the beach was empty, apart from them—and went on looking at Felicity, sounding surprised. 'I do believe I'd believe anything you told me.'

More fool you, she thought, and said, 'It doesn't pay to be too trusting,' and wondered, Why am I warning him? Deirdre took him on trust, she believed him.

'But there are remains of old buildings out there,' she said. 'I've swum down among them, although I didn't see any church bells.'

'I can imagine you doing that, drifting in and out of green caverns, your hair floating.' His voice was bantering, 'Mermaids must have eyes like yours.'

Drowning women have floating hair, she thought. 'How long have you been down here?' she asked.

'About a couple of weeks. I've been staying with friends.'

'Your friend was with us for a fortnight.' He threw the stick again for Sam and walked after it, and Felicity followed, picking up a piece of driftwood on the way, persisting, 'She's very beautiful. Is she special?'

'Yes,' he agreed, 'she is beautiful.'

Sam and Felicity reached him together, Sam panting, tail swishing, Felicity quiet now and waiting. 'And no,' he said, 'she is not a special friend, whatever she may have said.'

That was it. If she had had any doubts about the callous way he had treated Deirdre that did for them. Felicity began to fill her basket with less discrimination than usual, chattering, 'She didn't say much. She used to go for walks on her own, and she used to come down and wait for the post in the mornings. It seemed likely there was a man involved, and when you turned up, asking for her——' She wouldn't be able to carry the basket if she loaded it with any more stones, *and* she'd crush the shells. She sat down on her heels and started to discard some. 'I wondered if you were the man,' she said.

'For a while.'

'And it's over?'

'Quite over.'

'Then why did you come?'

'To talk to her,' he said. 'But I can't pretend I was sorry to hear she'd gone abroad.' He added drily, 'Anything else you'd like to know?'

She knew so much more about that affair than he dreamed. She had seen its bitter aftermath for Deirdre. She said, 'I'm asking too many questions,' and got up; she didn't feel comfortable kneeling at his feet. 'I always gather in too many pebbles,' she babbled, 'then I can't carry the basket.'

'Ask all the questions you want.' His eyes held hers and his were the colour of the storm clouds, and she lowered her lids because he wasn't getting into *her* head.

'Is there anything you'd like to know about me?' she asked, and he laughed a little, on the same note of surprise she had heard earlier.

'It's a strange thing, but I feel I know you very well.' Suddenly his hands were cupping her shoulders and he was studying her face with a concentration that made her breath catch. She was wearing a thick coat, but she felt his touch tingling through it. 'What I don't know I'll learn,' he said.

You will not, she thought, you will get no closer to me than this. But her lips were unsteady as though his mouth was coming down on hers, and she made them smile. 'Maybe,' she said. 'Maybe.'

They walked along the beach, most of the time in what would have been a pleasant silence with any other man. But Felicity couldn't forget for a moment how he had treated Deirdre, and now he thought he had Felicity whenever he wanted her, and that kept her nerves jangling.

He watched her foraging, with a smile lifting the corner of his mouth and deepening the lines beside his eyes, and sometimes she would smile slowly, as though being with him turned the cold and lonely beach into somewhere as warm and colourful as a South Sea island.

When they talked she knew the answers to give and the comments to make. Their tastes seemed to tally on everything, and added to this Felicity was flirting outrageously, turning on the full battery of her remarkable eyes as though she was finding him tremendously attractive. If it hadn't been for Deirdre she might have done, but, knowing what she did, she wouldn't have wanted David Holle if he had been the last man alive.

She was searching now for pink shells and small pink

pebbles, darting around the rocks, swift and graceful as a dancer. 'How long have you been making these?' David asked her.

'A few years. I used to work in an art shop, they sell them for me. I never went to art school.' She gave a deprecating grimace, 'Well, they're just a bit of tat really, aren't they? I try to make them into pretty patterns and it all helps subsidise the guest-house. Oh, *Sam*,' she shrieked, 'get *away*!'

Sam, tired of retrieving sticks, had just finished investigating a rock pool and rushed back to shake himself all over her.

'Suppose the guest-house doesn't pay,' David enquired, 'what will you do then?'

She had been trying to dodge Sam, but at that she stood stock still. 'It must,' she said, because there was no other way she could afford to go on living here. Gordon was always telling her she could end up having to sell up, and she expected that from Gordon, who had his reasons. But what right had David Holle to voice the fear that haunted her, and she turned on him with a set jaw and eyes blazing with determination. 'It will be a success—I'll make it a success. Nothing is going to drive me away. My family have lived in that house for ever!'

This time there was no sweetness in her smile, it was glinting and angry. 'I'll make it pay,' she said, 'no matter what it takes; and don't be fooled by my size, because I'm as tough a lady as you'll ever come across.'

She had never blazed out like that before. She had shrugged off Gordon's pessimism, and stayed cheerful with Mrs Clemo and Jessie, reminding them that this was only their first season and it all took time. But David Holle's casual query seemed to have struck a raw nerve, triggering a violence that left her shaking.

He said nothing. Swooping seabirds screeched above and she could have thrown back her head and screamed with them. She said at last, 'I must be more scared than I thought. I really didn't think I was scared at all because things are not going badly. I'm breaking even, nearly, and that's a fair start, and I'm only just starting.'

He took a step towards her and she thought, he's going to put his arms around me, and I can do without his comforting—look where it got Deirdre.

She forced brightness into her voice and started to walk back towards the causeway. 'That's my home you see, and this,' indicating the beach and the basket of shells and pebbles, 'is my garden, and I'm fond of the old place. If it should ever fall into the sea I'll go down with it.' She laughed at him, over her shoulder, 'And live in cool green rooms, like a mermaid.'

'But you're not a mermaid.' His voice was as light as her own. 'Mermaids don't have beautiful legs.'

'Haven't you heard of evolution?'

'If this is the end result I'm all for it. Can I carry your basket?'

'Stones weigh heavy,' she said as she handed it over, and he nodded.

'You're right, you *are* a tough lady.'

But not as tough as you, Felicity thought, and I don't have time to be playing games. When we get back I shall tell you about Deirdre and from then on I'll stick to the business of running a guest-house.

Mrs Clemo was polishing a table in the lounge when they went in, and tutted as Sam left a trail of wet over the flagstones, 'You should have brought that dog in by the other door.' The kitchen door was up a steep flight of rock steps, rarely used, but it was a long time since Sam had run berserk on the beach and Mrs Clemo, remembering, sighed. 'I used to say that to the Captain.' She looked at Sam with less disapproval. 'He's brightened up, hasn't he?'

'Perhaps it's dawned on him that we're running a business here,' said Felicity, 'and he's starting to welcome the guests.'

'Perhaps he thinks this one's here for a nice long stay,' Mrs Clemo beamed at David, who said, 'He could be right.'

'Miss Mayne tells me you're a writer.' Mrs Clemo sensed a long-term customer. 'Now this could be just the place for somebody like you. Peace and quiet, and it's beautiful round here, a real inspiration this place could be. Did you see an ad or were we recommended?'

'No, I——' David began, and Felicity said hastily,

'Could I trouble you to carry these up to the office, then I can get on with sorting them?'

There was no reason why Mrs Clemo shouldn't know that he had come looking for Deirdre, but Felicity would prefer to get her say in first. In her private room she would tell him that Deirdre was an old friend and she would rather that David Holle did not hang around. Lord knows she needed the rooms filled, but he was one customer she could manage without.

She walked into her room ahead of him, took half a dozen paces, turned and was in his arms. She had expected him to put down the basket and stand, not march right after her and envelop her in a bear-hug that scooped her off her feet. She croaked and he put her down again and she gulped in air.

'Sorry,' he said, 'but I've wanted to do that all morning.'

She had been giving him come-hither looks all morning, so she only had herself to blame, but she said tartly, 'Do what? Break my ribs?' He hadn't hurt her, it had just been a hug, but it had made her realise how big he was, and how strong. If he had decided that she had really been signalling an invitation to go all the way she wouldn't have stood a cat in hell's chance. *And* she had just asked him up to her bedroom, although the bed was a divan by day, the bedclothes stacked discreetly away.

'This is my *office*,' she said.

'So it is.' He was humouring her.

'And my workroom, that shelf.'

'Yes.'

'You don't know your own strength, do you?' She was getting her breath back, but that closeness had been as disturbing as an attempted rape; although he hadn't even kissed her, just held her against him.

'I thought I did. I've never broken any ribs before.' He was smiling, but then the smile went. 'Is it that bad?'

'What?'

'Business.'

After that outburst on the beach just now she had stopped playing teasing games, and walked back here, and they hadn't done much more talking. He must have thought she was worried. She said, 'No—really. I told you, it's going to be fine. I'm not out to make a fortune anyway, just keep the place going, and I can't think why I'm discussing it with you.'

'May I see your books?' he asked, unexpectedly.

They didn't make thrilling reading, but it *was* early days. She was standing by her desk, the account books were in a drawer, and she had no intention of letting this man inspect them. The very idea! But there was a compelling authority about him. He was hard and ruthless beneath that veneer of easy charm, but perhaps a hard and brilliant mind might come up with some bright ideas. 'Why?' she asked.

'I'd like to help you put the place on the map. I enjoy

a challenge.' Deirdre had told Felicity that and she was intrigued.

'And what would you suggest?' she asked.

'Spending some money.'

But she was stretched to her limits. Her grandfather's little legacy and a bank loan had covered two more bathrooms and a modernised kitchen, equipment, insurance, all manner of things. She gave an infinitesimal shrug and grimace, indicating that there was the rub. 'Whose money?'

'Mine,' he said, and she stared with surprise, wondering how far he would go with this. Perhaps he did see possibilities in the business. If so it could do no harm to hear them.

She said, 'You've got money to spare? There's not many can say that these days.'

'I earn enough for my needs.' His needs seemed to be those of a very successful man. His clothes were casual but well cut, expensive, you could tell. Then there was the powerful car and the London flat with its antiques and the Turner in the living room. Deirdre had said he was generous, a big spender. 'With a little over,' he added. 'May I see the books?'

Felicity had nothing to hide. It was all straightforward. 'Why not?' She took two account books out of the drawer and put them on the desk, and he came round, sat down, and opened one. 'Do you understand it?' she asked.

'Yes.'

'Right, then, have a read.' She had a sensation of losing control, of things happening that were not to her liking. She stood for a moment, biting her thumb, then she walked across to where he had put down the basket by her work shelf, and began to take out the contents. She didn't look towards the desk again. She arranged pebbles and shells in size and colour, although it was a waste of time before they were polished and treated. She was pretending to be busy because she couldn't just stand there, watching him. Pity she couldn't make a sea-spell for herself, to lure the customers in.

She heard him close a book, then he said, 'You can do better than this.' He sounded like a schoolteacher making an end-of-term report.

'Can do better,' she shrugged. 'Does not try hard enough. But I *do* try. I work, I tell you. I can't go out and drag 'em in. And I suppose it is a bad time to be opening a guest-house.'

This was the first time she had admitted that even super hotels were feeling the pinch, and the bed-and-breakfasts had 'Vacancies' up more often than not.

'Not necessarily,' he said. 'How do you get your customers? You advertise, obviously. Where?'

Felicity named newspapers. 'And recommendations,' she said. 'And they do come back. One man's been twice already this year, and I had a letter the other day saying he was hoping to get over for another weekend soon.'

'A very satisfied customer,' David drawled, and she looked at him sharply,

'It's the food,' she explained, and then, 'Well, of course I try to make them feel at home. Now if I were a mermaid I could sit on the rocks and sing a siren song and lure them in.'

'Now there,' he said, 'we might have something.'

'Not with my voice. Seriously, do you have any suggestions?'

'One obvious improvement is the causeway. I wonder nobody's slipped on that before now and sued you.'

'Could they?'

'It's debatable. We might find out at which stage it

ceases to be the responsibility of the local authorities and starts being part of Gull Rock House.'

'I don't think I want to think about this,' she said. 'I have problems, don't I?' She began to spin the old globe of the world, slowly. Nearly everybody who came into this room did that. 'Not to mention,' she went on, 'that we're into the season of high tides when we can get cut off. And storms, of course. We're famous for them round here.'

She was still spinning the globe, looking down at it, but she saw him get up and come to her, and he put a hand over hers, stilling the spinning. 'This house could be the eye of the storm,' he said. 'The centre, where it's quiet and safe.' His hand covered hers and beneath it she pressed her fingers down. She didn't feel safe, she felt threatened, and when he moved away it was as though he released her. She moved too, putting the account books back in the drawer, staying behind the desk and keeping it between them although he wasn't looking her way now.

'The food is excellent,' David said. 'The wine list's adequate.'

'I'm trying to specialise in Cornish cooking.'

'Good. Yes. Get yourself known for your own specialities.' He was pacing the room, looking around, seeking inspiration. 'Good food and service will bring them back, but we need to get them here in the first place.'

'I'm in an overcrowded business,' Felicity said ruefully, 'with nothing to give me the edge over the rest.'

'Nonsense!' his denial was explosive. 'This place is unique. There can't be many to touch it for atmosphere. We need publicity, I can get you a write-up here and there, and we must make the readers want to come and see for themselves where it all happened.'

'Where what happened?' She was being carried along, agog to hear what was coming next.

'The village under the sea?' He was throwing out suggestions, then he winced. 'No, they might start wondering if this house is due to join it. And that's another thing, I'd be happier if I was sure the building was safe. Although I suppose they went into all that before you got a licence?' She nodded. 'Was it wrecker country?' he asked. 'Or how about smuggling?'

'Smuggling all along the coast. Wrecking probably, but Tregorran Cove never made a name that way.'

'Who are all these?'

All her photographs. 'My family,' she explained. 'I brought them in here for company.' Since her grandfather died she had been lonely, in spite of friends, in spite of Gordon.

'Your grandfather was the Captain?'

'Yes.' She picked up a snapshot, in a small silver frame, that she had taken when she was trying out a new camera not long before he died. He was standing on the rocks outside the house, pipe in his mouth, white-bearded and rugged, looking good for another ten years, although he had been nearly eighty.

'Was this his room?'

'Yes.'

'You could turn it into your best room—the Captain's Room. The other bedrooms are comfortable and attractive, I'm sure, but this has to be in a class of its own.'

'But I don't want to move out of here,' she protested, and he shrugged and she said, 'Well, I suppose I could make do with something smaller.'

'Who was she?'

Now he was standing in front of the sepia

daguerreotype of the young woman in the high-necked dress, wearing the seed-pearl brooch. 'My grandfather's grandmother,' said Felicity. 'Carlotta, the sea-witch.'

'The what?'

She had expected that to catch him. 'Over a hundred years ago folk were superstitious, especially in Cornwall, and she turned up in Tregorran Cove, unconscious on the beach after a storm. A ship had gone down with all hands, and she was Spanish so nobody could understand a word she said, and she was hurt and she stayed in this house, being nursed back to health and falling in love with young Willie Mayne who'd found her. There was trouble because he was supposed to be marrying a local girl, only after the sea-witch was washed up everyone said he was bewitched.' She smiled, this was a family legend that had been passed on. 'There was uproar in the church because of her foreign accent. When she was repeating her marriage vows half the congregation thought it was devil-talk, but she and Willie were declared man and wife.'

'And?' David prompted as she paused.

'And they lived happily, I think, but she always had a name for second sight and fortune-telling and making things go her way. I suppose that's why I call my shell things sea-spells.'

'You're descended from her, of course?'

'Of course.'

'There we are, then. This isn't just your run-of-the-mill guest-house. This is the home of the sea-witch, and her living, breathing great-great-granddaughter. Anyone staying here and going home with a sea-spell will be lucky.'

It was a selling point that should have occurred to her. She had concentrated on making the place comfortable and the food memorable. But he was right, the house had character, and she should have been capitalising on that too. She knew that her ancestress had been a beautiful girl from a foreign land, entirely human, but a tale of myth and magic could surely be spun.

'We need a painting of her,' David decided.

'From the photograph?' It was faded, but the features were still clear. 'I know some artists who do traditional portraits.'

'Get someone to paint the Captain. He'll look well in here. And are any of these William?'

Felicity pointed to another daguerreotype farther along the wall. 'He was in the same album on the page facing her—my grandfather said he was her husband.' She would enjoy seeing paintings of these faded photographs, but she wondered how she would feel, faced with a life-sized portrait of her grandfather.

'I'd like to do the sea-witch myself,' said David.

'Are you any good?'

Deirdre had said he was, of course, and remembering Deirdre reminded Felicity that this was the last man she would choose as a partner. She wouldn't touch his money, she couldn't bear to actually owe him, but the right publicity could be better than any advertisement, and he would know how to organise that, so she couldn't send him away just yet.

She would hang the portrait of Carlotta somewhere in the lounge, where it could be seen as soon as guests came into the house. 'I'm reckoned a fair amateur,' David was saying, 'and I've got a feeling about this one,' but he was looking at Felicity.

'You're going to paint her like me, aren't you?'

'She is like you.'

She had always known that among all the old

photographs this was the face nearest her own, but she would rather someone else was painting the picture. And they could if she didn't like David Holle's efforts when she saw them. For now she could hardly object. 'How long would it take?' she asked. 'Can you spare the time?'

'I'm working on a script with a Cornish background. I planned to stay in the area for a month or two and, as the lady downstairs pointed out, this could be the ideal place.'

'Because you need peace and quiet?' Her eyebrows arched. 'That was Mrs Clemo's sales talk. I told you, the weather gets tough.'

'Did I say I was looking for peace and quiet?'

'What are you looking for?' she had enquired before she could stop herself, and when he took a step towards her her stomach muscles clenched in panic. She was scared he was going to take hold of her again, but he went to the desk and the photograph of Gordon, and asked, 'Is this one family too?'

'No, that one is a friend.'

'How good a friend?' He meant, was the man her lover? and with his record how had he got the nerve to question any girl like this?

'*Very* good.' She made it emphatic, and he put Gordon's picture face down, as if that disposed of Gordon, and she didn't know whether to laugh or blow her top at his presumption. Then he said, 'You haven't asked if I'm married.'

Deirdre said he wasn't. Felicity began, 'If you are——'

'I'm not,' he said, 'which is just as well.'

'Why is it just as well?'

He had undeniable magnetism. Some peculiar fusion happened when they faced each other like this.

'Because, whoever she was, I'd have difficulty in remembering her when I looked at you,' he said quietly, and for a moment Felicity couldn't remember Gordon's face either. Then she stood the photograph up again because she must not forget Gordon, nor Deirdre; and she must seriously consider whether, if she let this man stay under her roof, she could keep his hands off her until he had served his purpose and she could send him on his way.

CHAPTER FOUR

MRS CLEMO was in the kitchen, putting the carpet sweeper back in the broom cupboard, when Felicity came downstairs, and Felicity closed the kitchen door and said, 'I've got something I want to discuss with you. I want your advice.'

In fact she had already made up her mind and she didn't anticipate any objections, but the three women worked in happy harmony and of course Felicity wanted to keep it that way. 'David Holle has some ideas about this place,' she said, and got all Mrs Clemo's startled attention.

'You don't mean he wants to buy it?'

'*No*, you know I'd never sell.' Not while there was any legal way of staying on. 'But he will be in Cornwall for a while and he thinks he might stay here, that he could write here, and the house interests him. He says we ought to be making more of it, not just offering good food and comfortable beds but creating atmosphere by putting pictures of the family around. After all, it's always been a family home, hasn't it?'

Mrs Clemo nodded, and Felicity continued, 'He thinks that we should call my grandfather's old room the Captain's Room and let guests stay in it, with the charts and the maps and the telescope and the globe, and perhaps have a painting done of my grandfather. We could charge extra, of course.'

Mrs Clemo went on nodding, so far this seemed reasonable. 'And another painting of his grandmother,' added Felicity.

'Oh,' said Mrs Clemo. 'That one!' No question which grandmother, although Rachel Clemo had been born years after Carlotta Mayne's death. As a child she had heard the stories, and for all her down-to-earth manner she was as superstitious as her forebears.

'They called her the sea-witch, didn't they?' Felicity was full of plans now. 'My grandfather used to tell me about her, and I'm sure there are letters and papers in those boxes in the attic. Well,' as she got no response, 'don't you think it's a good idea? She'll be a talking point, something the other guest-houses don't have.'

'I don't know as we want her either,' said Mrs Clemo sharply. 'By all accounts she was best left alone.'

'But you don't *believe* it?' Felicity had to laugh. 'Oh, come on, you know it was all prejudice and imagination in those days. Now it would just be a gimmick. Times have changed.'

'Maybe,' retorted Mrs Clemo, 'but folk haven't.'

'They have everywhere else but here,' said Felicity. 'I agree there hasn't been much progress around Tregorran Cove in the last two hundred years, but if changing our image will bring in the customers then I've got to try it, because——' hearing her own words made her heart sink as if she was listening to somebody else, 'because I'm scared I'm not going to make this place pay, the way I'm going on.'

She had never said she was scared before today. Today she had admitted it twice, once on the beach to David, and now. 'He can help us get publicity,' she said. 'Help put us on the map.'

Talking with him, upstairs in her room, had refuelled her initial excitement and enthusiasm. It could all be done during the winter months, when there was no passing trade and she might as well shut down.

'What did bring him here?' asked Mrs Clemo abruptly. 'I can see you're taken with him, and he looks at you a bit old-fashioned. He's no stranger, is he?'

'Yes and no,' said Felicity. Coffee was percolating, Mrs Clemo had turned it on as soon as Felicity and David Holle returned from the beach, and Felicity poured two cups now and said, 'Sit down and have a cup while I tell you the rest of it.'

Mrs Clemo expected to hear something that was going to put Gordon Stretton's nose out of joint. She wouldn't have minded that, the way he kept on about the guest-house being a lost cause, but what Felicity was telling her sounded ominous.

'I'd never seen him before he turned up last night, but I had heard of him. He came to see if Deirdre was still here. They'd been very close until he decided he wanted to finish.'

'I knew it!' Mrs Clemo couldn't resist her little triumph. 'I knew that what ailed that poor girl was a man. Well, this isn't much of a reason for putting much faith in him.'

'This would be business,' said Felicity, quickly and emphatically. 'Knowing what happened to Deirdre, of course, I'd only trust him in business matters, I'd *never* get emotionally involved.'

Mrs Clemo continued to look dubious, and Felicity wondered if she was recalling how they had come in from that walk on the beach together. That might have looked like the start of a relationship that was not entirely business.

'One other thing,' she said, 'and please don't tell anybody but Jessie.'

Jessie was like her mother in many ways, except that at twenty-five Jessie was livelier and still good for a giggle. But neither gossiped, both could keep a secret, and Felicity went on, 'He doesn't know that Deirdre and I went to school together and I invited her down here. He thinks she just came, saw an advertisement or somebody told her about us, and she came because we're not too far from Padstow where he was staying. And I didn't tell him any different.'

Mrs Clemo was sitting back in her chair, arms folded, frowning a strained scowl of concentration. 'Why didn't you?'

'Well,' Felicity took a deep breath because this was going to take some explaining, 'first of all I thought I'd lead him on to pay him for the way he'd treated her. She was on the edge of a nervous breakdown when she came here, you know, and it was all through him. She just couldn't think about anything else, nor talk about anything else—not to me, at any rate. The things I know about that man!'

She grinned, but Mrs Clemo did not. Several expressions had flitted across Mrs Clemo's face, but her frown had stayed constant. 'He thinks it's weird the way I can tune in to his wavelength,' said Felicity. 'He thinks I'm incredible, and this morning I was going to tell him to clear off, but then he began talking about getting us some publicity, and writing the story up for us, and he's quite a famous writer and it would get Gull Rock House off to a good start and we do need all the help we can get. So I thought, well, let him, why not?'

The reason why not was obvious, he had almost broken Deirdre's heart. But in the end Deirdre had come through, and he was making a business offer that Felicity would find it hard to refuse.

'Is he going to charge you?' demanded Mrs Clemo.

'No.'

'What's he expecting for it?'

That Felicity would be sharing his bed, and she shrivelled at the thought and said fiercely, 'I'll tell you what he'll get—board and lodgings on fair terms and damn all else. Don't worry, I can handle it.'

'She was small, you know, like you,' said Mrs Clemo abruptly, talking about Carlotta as though she had seen her. 'They said she could call up the storms. Watch out that you don't.'

Felicity's grandfather had said that one day she would call up a storm, when she first brought Gordon home. Felicity had laughed then and she tried to laugh now. 'No need to call 'em up, is there? Not on this coast.' But neither Mrs Clemo nor her grandfather had been talking about the weather. They had both meant that she might release some primitive and destructive force that she could no longer control. 'Coffee's getting cold,' said Felicity.

She hadn't touched hers yet, and after one sip Mrs Clemo had lost interest in coffee. Now Felicity sat down at the table too and both women drank in silence. Mrs Clemo had plenty to think about, Felicity had said all she could say for the moment. Mrs Clemo could wreck the project of the sea-witch if she had a mind to. Well, not wreck it entirely, Felicity could still use David Holle's suggestion, but his writing skill and his publicity connections would be invaluable.

He would be walking into the kitchen any minute.

She had left him upstairs and said, 'I'll go and have a word with Mrs Clemo about this. I wouldn't even choose a wallpaper without her approval.'

It was nearly true. She was very fond of Mrs Clemo and always listened to her opinions. She would have been unlikely to select a wallpaper that Mrs Clemo hated—this house had been Mrs Clemo's second home since Felicity was a child—but on important matters she made up her own mind.

Now she sat, sipping her coffee and musing. The kitchen and the bathrooms were the only rooms in the house that Great-great-grandmother Carlotta would not have recognised. She would have cooked in here, with an open fire and side ovens, but that was too domesticated to feature in her story. A sea-witch should be exotic, mysterious, spooky. Perhaps they could turn one of the bedrooms into her special room. A small room maybe, facing the sea, of course. She chose one, and in her mind's eye began to refurnish it with selected pieces.

When David Holle walked into the kitchen she jumped and smiled, explaining, 'Just doing some planning.' He put a light hand caressingly on her shoulder, and she hated him touching her. She stood up and went to the percolator to pour him some coffee, but she could still feel the weight of his hand. 'Mrs Clemo thinks that Great-great-grandmama is best left alone,' she said.

Some of the disapproval on Mrs Clemo's face was probably for the way David Holle had treated Deirdre. She was quite capable of saying now, 'I hear you knew that poor young Deirdre,' and Felicity held her breath. But when Mrs Clemo did speak she said, 'There've always been Maynes in this house and I wouldn't like to see it go out of the family. Nor would the Captain.' Her loyalty was to the Maynes. Mrs Clemo, thank goodness, was keeping mum.

. 'It won't go to strangers,' said Felicity, sounding confident again, although the doubt was always in her heart. She put the coffee on the table by David and gave Mrs Clemo a hug. 'You'll back me up, won't you, like you always do?'

'Oh yes,' said Mrs Clemo, 'like I always do.' She looked at David Holle with grudging sympathy, 'I don't know about sea-witches, but if this one sets her mind on something she could coax the devil himself into helping her.'

Felicity gave a yelp of protest and mock horror. 'Oh *no*, that gentleman's fee for services might come too high,' adding mischievously, 'Mind you, if he came after lodgings and promised to act in a civilised fashion I might just take him in.'

'Devil's promises,' muttered Mrs Clemo.

'Like piecrust,' said Felicity gaily, 'made to be broken.' She turned dancing eyes on David. 'And she isn't joking.'

'Neither am I.' He addressed himself to Mrs Clemo, serious and persuasive. 'The competition in small hotels is cut-throat these days. You're offering good value, but you still need something extra, and Carlotta could be a real attraction. If I'm writing her story I shall treat her with respect. I don't believe in witches, but I do believe there are more things in heaven and earth——'

'That's what I say,' said Mrs Clemo, who had never quoted *Hamlet* in her life, but was being reassured now by David Holle's manner. The strong clean-cut features, the quiet voice and the relaxed stance, all conveyed confidence; and Felicity could have put her own trust in him unconditionally if she hadn't known that that was Deirdre's undoing. Although of course it was falling in love that was Deirdre's mistake. In business matters Felicity thought he would probably keep his word.

'Well, if it brings in the customers I suppose it'll be all right,' Mrs Clemo conceded. 'I'll be getting on with it,' meaning the chores. 'What about lunch?'

There would only be David and Felicity today, so Felicity suggested, 'How about us going into Fenmouth and getting lunch there? We could take the photographs to show to a couple who might do the paintings. I'd like you to see their work.'

He agreed readily, as she was sure he would go along with anything within reason that she suggested. Men usually did, but David Holle was no ordinary susceptible male. He was sensual and cynical and his infatuation would be brief. As soon as she made it plain that sex was not on the agenda she would lose most of her hold over him.

'Carlotta seems to be something of a local celebrity,' he said as they walked up the staircase, back to Felicity's room.

'Not really. Mrs Clemo was remembering old tales she must have heard years ago. Cornwall has always been heavy on superstition and she was reminding me just now that times might change but down here folk don't.'

'Folk don't change anywhere,' he said. 'When you reach bedrock the most powerful human forces are always love and hate.'

Felicity paused to straighten a flower print on the wall as they walked along the corridor, talking for talking's sake. 'Love and hate are said to be hard to tell apart. What do you think?'

'I hope not,' he said quietly. 'Loving your enemy could rip your heart out.'

If you had a heart. 'Have you done much hating?' She wouldn't ask about loving.

'No,' he said, 'but I've seen too much—I was a war correspondent.' She hadn't known that, Deirdre hadn't mentioned it.

'That must have been——' She couldn't find words to express how terrible that must have been, and as she hesitated he said briefly,

'Yes,' and in a lighter tone, closing that subject, 'Have you done much loving?'

'Depends what you mean by loving.' They had reached her room. 'I love this house,' she ran the back of her hand down a wall. 'But if you mean how many men have I slept with the answer to that's none of your business.'

'True.' But from now on he was making it his business, the glint of his smile told her that, and she started talking again, fast.

'There are trunks full of papers in the attics, we might be able to find some from Carlotta's time, and things like old bills, old letters might even be worth framing.'

'They might indeed.' He had gone over again to the portrait of Carlotta, studying it closely, the way he had looked at Felicity's face on the beach. 'She's wearing a brooch,' he said.

Felicity opened a drawer and took out an old red leather-covered jewellery box. It was a far from fabulous collection, but there were some pretty pieces that had come down to her, and she picked out a small antique seed-pearl bar. 'My grandfather said this was hers. It isn't very clear in the photograph, but I've always thought this was the one it had to be.'

She pinned the pin on her sweater, at the throat. She had always liked it, she wore it sometimes, but if David was featuring it in the painting she would wear it constantly. She said, 'I had another idea—you know what you were saying about this being the Captain's

Room? Well, I thought that we should have Carlotta's room too. It wouldn't be cheating, they were all her rooms once, but we could make one of the bedrooms special, put the right period furniture in, a chair at the window on which she sat and looked out over the sea.'

'Why not?'

She fingered the seed-pearl bar. 'I'd half decided on a room, shall I show you? Or maybe you'll think one of the others would be better.' She wanted to consult him because the more involved he became the more help he would give. 'If I'm wearing her brooch,' she said, 'maybe I'll get the right vibrations when we reach the right room.'

She wasn't serious about that, she smiled as she spoke, coming out on to the landing again. 'Only the rooms with a sea view,' she said. Upstairs, apart from the Captain's Room, the rooms were small, and she opened the first door, walked in and wandered around, with graceful fluid movements, eyes wide, head turning as she listened. 'Great-great-grandmama,' she intoned, 'how did you feel about this room?'

David leaned against the door-jamb, arms folded, smiling at her performance, and acting jokey was the easiest way of being with him. 'I get no message,' said Felicity, after a few moments.

'What were you expecting, one knock for yes, two for no?'

She was expecting nothing, of course, and neither was he, but she went from room to room. His photograph was still in that drawer in the room that Deirdre had used, and when he opened that door for her she shook her head. 'Not that one, no. I rather fancied this.'

She led him to the room she had almost settled on before she started this pantomime, a corner room, much like the rest, with pretty wallpaper and old-fashioned furniture. 'Yes,' she said, stepping inside, 'Oh yes, I have the feeling here that this was where she used to look over the sea, where the houses are under the waves and the church bells still ring.'

She brushed against him. Her hand caught his hand, or he caught hers, and she was in his arms, and she felt the shock of his mouth as piercing and deep as though he took complete possession of her. For seconds she was on fire. Then she was ice, blood draining from her cheeks, from every inch of her skin that had been burning a moment ago, and she struggled against him and he drew back, still holding her, looking down at her.

'What is it?' he asked. 'What's the matter?'

'I——' her tongue flickered between lips that felt swollen and bruised, although they were not.

'You look like death,' David said. 'Sit down—here.' He put her into a ladder-backed rush-seated chair by the window, and bent over her, chafing one of her hands between his because it was suddenly clammy cold.

'What's the matter?' he asked her again, and she couldn't give him the true explanation, 'You kissed me and this is a case of sick-to-the-stomach revulsion.' She pressed her hand across her mouth and mumbled, 'I t-told you—I s-suddenly felt I was getting through to her,' stammering on, 'Perhaps it is the brooch. Do you believe in that sort of thing?'

'No.' He was still rubbing her hand, gently, but she wished he would stop. 'But then I didn't believe in witches until I met you.'

Felicity was getting her wits back and her blood had started to flow again. 'I don't really believe in it either,' she said, 'But I always did have this over-active imagination.'

'I'll buy that.' Now he had let go of her. 'I wouldn't like to think it was anything to do with me.'

He had used her friend despicably, but she needed his help and she said very slowly, 'What are you expecting to get out of this?'

'Why are you asking?'

Now she was rubbing her own fingers, lacing and twisting them. 'Because I wouldn't like to give you the wrong idea, about me, about us. I'm grateful for your interest, I think it's a very good idea to give this place a character of its own, and I'd love you to stay here.' Her lips twitched and she hoped it looked like a smile. 'On special terms. But I can't cope with any kind of—er— physical involvements. Friends, yes, that would be lovely, that I would be very happy about, but—er——' She floundered and David said,

'No sex, thank you.'

'You've got it.'

'On the contrary.' He smiled at her and she had to smile back. Well, she had told him. If he stayed on these terms he couldn't complain he had been cheated.

'You see, there's Gordon,' she explained.

'Yes, there is Gordon.'

'No offence meant.' She managed to make that sound apologetic and appealing.

'None taken.' He looked grave, but there was still laughter in his voice. 'Not offence nor anything else.'

'You do understand?'

'Certainly.'

'And I've got your word on it?' She was labouring the point. She didn't need to keep on.

'Of course.' It was all too easy. He was being too obliging. Devil's promises, she thought, made to be broken; and she knew that whatever he said she wouldn't trust him. But she would have to pretend she did and hope that she could keep the situation under control.

She said, 'That's all right, then. So shall we take the photographs into Fenmouth?'

The tide was coming in, lapping the sides of the causeway, and now it had been pointed out to her she noticed how uneven the great stones were, the slippery patches of moss and weed. She even seemed less surefooted herself today because she was watching every step instead of striding on with her usual confidence. Once, when she stumbled, David put out a hand which she ignored. She didn't want him imagining she was doing this on purpose, she had no intention of continuing hand in hand or arm in arm.

The beach was deserted and the few people on the sea-front were hurrying about their business. Jan Tregeagle, Jessie's husband, broad-shouldered and black-bearded as a pirate and one of the gentlest of men, hailed Felicity as she walked into the boatyard. He was replacing a rotting board in an upturned dinghy and they had a few words about the weather.

White-capped rollers were breaking against the rocks and the wind was rising. 'Gale force before night,' Jan forecast, and Felicity agreed. She introduced David, 'Who'll be staying with us for a while,' and Jan as, 'Mrs Clemo's son-in-law.' The two men were much of a height—and that, Felicity reflected, was about all they did have in common. 'We're off into Fenmouth,' she said. 'Tell Jessie I'll see her later. Her mother has some news for her.'

Her smile had to include David, and Jan said, 'Has she now?' considering what the news, concerning Felicity and the man who was smiling down at her and would be 'staying with us for a while', was likely to be. 'She never did think much of Gordon Stretton's chances,' he chuckled, and Felicity coloured and snapped,

'About the guest-house, you great pillock!' but Jan went on grinning.

'Perceptive chap,' remarked David as they reached the parking spaces reserved for Gull Rock House.

'Usually,' Felicity admitted. 'Not this time, and I can't imagine why he said that about Gordon, because I'm sure Jessie didn't.'

'Were you going to marry him?' Not *are* you? Just taking it for granted that any matrimonial plans she might have had had changed since she met him. The arrogance of the man! 'Why?' she enquired sweetly, 'Are you suggesting I should marry you?'

She expected to shake him, but of course he took it as a joke, tossing it back to her, asking 'What do you think?'

'I think you'd be out of your mind if you did,' she said promptly, 'and I don't think you're out of your mind. Are we taking my van?'

'Would you mind if we took the car?'

'Not a bit. I love a stylish ride.'

Van and car stood side by side. The flight of white gulls painted across the blue of the van had been an eye-catching advertisement for Gull Rock House, and now she stood back a little, surveying it, wondering, 'Should we change this? Should we get the sea-witch into it?'

He viewed it with her. 'Maybe a silhouette. A girl standing on the rocks.'

'Mmm.' Felicity climbed into the car when he opened the door, and sank into the passenger seat still looking at the van. She didn't want to look at him. It was a big car, but he was a big man and she was closed in with him, and if she turned he would probably smile and he could easily touch her, kiss her. So she made a show of looking out for obstacles, and waving cheerio to Jan, and kept well to her own side of the car until they were turning from the sea-front to climb the hill to the cliff top road and David Holle was fully occupied.

The conversation went along similar lines as Felicity's chat to Deirdre, driving this route to the same destination nearly three weeks ago. She had tried to catch Deirdre's attention by telling her about the artists who lived and worked in Trevarrow's Yard, but Deirdre had hardly heard a word. That was the difference; David listened, showing real interest. At the end of her ride with Deirdre Felicity had felt quite drained and depressed, but David Holle kept her pepped up. Perhaps it *was* tension, but the adrenalin certainly flowed while he was around.

Trevarrow's Yard was a cul-de-sac round a cobbled courtyard. The original Tom Trevarrow had been a Victorian merchant who lived in a big house with outbuildings and warehouses. Over the years the house, on the main road, had been converted into offices and a café, while the buildings behind had become shops, homes, workrooms and studios. Trevarrow's Yard was now an artists' community and Felicity knew most of them.

Parking was easier today. Some shops in the town were shut for the off-season, and there were shutters closed here and there in the Yard. But the shop Felicity was making for—cutting through a 'crack' from the main road—still had Open on the door.

The window displayed framed watercolours of local views, some original oil paintings and a charming collection of child miniatures in pastel shades. A bell jangled over the door as Felicity stepped in, and a man stood up from behind a table at the back of the shop.

He was small and wiry, with longish hair, receding at the front, and a nose that twisted slightly and made him look rather sinister.

'Felicity!' he flung his arms around her. 'You couldn't be more welcome if you were a customer!'

'Funny you should say that,' she said.

He gave David, standing just behind her, an amiable nod and called towards the iron spiral staircase that led up from the shop, 'It's Felicity!'

'Good-oh, come on up!' a female voice called down.

Felicity made for the staircase, doing the introductions as she went. 'Arthur Penrose, David Holle.'

'*The* David Holle?' That was what Felicity had said, but she had been putting on an act while Arthur seemed genuinely impressed. She stopped half way up the staircase to look down at the two men and add, 'He writes for T.V.'

'I know that,' said Arthur Penrose.

'Just thought I'd mention it,' said Felicity.

The staircase came up into a studio that filled almost the whole of the upper storey, and was always in a state of disarray. There was a black iron stove in the middle, an area devoted to Arthur's oil paintings, another where Marguerite created her miniatures, the kitchen in a corner, and various desks and tables and chairs and sofas, which were moved around from time to time when Marguerite decided to redesign her home.

Margie, plump, pretty and in her late twenties, was waiting at the top of the stairs. She was a talented artist, her portraits were little masterpieces of fine brushwork and delicate detail, but to look at her you would have thought that wall murals would be more in her line. Even when she was standing still she gave the impression of being caught in a high wind. Her dark hair, which she wore loose, was always untidy; buttons strained down the front of a cardigan that had probably shrunk in the wash; and more often than not she was breathless.

'This is lovely,' she said. 'You haven't been round in ages. I am glad you came, I'm having a rotten day.'

'What so rotten about it?' Felicity enquired, stepping off the top of the staircase on to the floorboards, and Margie pulled a face.

'This miserable weather. There's nobody about, and I'm fed up.' She had presumed Felicity was alone, when David appeared through the floorboards she said, 'Why, *hello*,' so enthusiastically that Felicity had to smile.

'This is David Holle.' Arthur had followed them.

'I say!' Margie rolled her eyes at Felicity. 'You never said you knew David Holle.'

'You are famous, aren't you?' Felicity had really not realised that. She had no television, reception was poor in Tregorran Cove, the cliffs had something to do with it, and an aerial wouldn't have lasted long on the roof of Gull Rock House.

'Don't you believe it,' said David. He took the two strides which got him to Felicity and stood by her while she told him Marguerite's name, and Margie said archly, 'Margie to my friends—and how long have you two been friends?'

'Less than twenty-four hours,' said Felicity. 'I meet a nice class of people, running a guest-house.'

The Penroses were always glad to see her. They were fond of Felicity, with her sparkle and vivacity, but David Holle overshadowed her. There was something about him that got everything together. Within minutes they were all gathered around the stove, on which a log was burning. Outside the wind was howling, but inside, right now, life seemed to have taken a turn for the better.

Felicity had deliberately seated herself on a cushion on the floor, because Margie and Arthur had left the sofa for her and David and she didn't want to be nestled up against him. But the warmth spread over her too, watching Arthur and Margie relaxing, talking, joking.

They were delighted at being included in the project of the sea-witch, and that was natural enough, a commission was a commission, but it wasn't only the money. Their imagination was caught, although until David and Felicity began to explain they had never heard of Carlotta.

'And we want an oil painting of my grandfather,' said Felicity. 'I've only got a snap of him, Arthur, but you do remember him, don't you? You did see him once or twice.'

Captain Mayne had come into town occasionally with Felicity, he had met the Penroses, and Arthur nodded, although he had only vague memories of a tall white-bearded old sailor.

Margie was given the photograph of William to copy as a miniature. 'I shall keep the originals on the wall in my room,' said Felicity. 'They did live in the house, they were all real people, we're not making them up—I'm not cheating, am I?'

'Certainly not,' said David, and she turned her face to the fire because she was cheating him and if she wasn't blushing she ought to be. She said, 'David's going to try painting Carlotta himself.'

'Do you have a picture of her?' Margie would have liked to see the woman they called a witch.

'We didn't bring it,' said Felicity.

'She was like Felicity,' said David, and Felicity didn't

want to look at him but she had to meet his eyes. She thought crazily, if I stretched out a hand he would get off that sofa and come to me, and if he reached I might not be able to stop myself going to him.

She began to chatter, managing to force a smile. 'She *was* my grandfather's grandmother, so I look a little like her faded photograph about the face. I've probably got the wrong hands and the wrong teeth. She was probably a great strapping wench.'

'Small, like you,' Mrs Clemo had told her. Margie said, 'There's always been something fey about you. I'll bet she was like you.' Margie was smiling and so was Arthur. And David. But the laughter wasn't in David's eyes. Although perhaps Felicity imagined that, because the visit to the Penroses was highly enjoyable.

Arthur shut the shop, there weren't going to be any customers in this weather, and Margie stretched a chili con carne she had been preparing for lunch with a pinch of powder, corned beef, and a tin of beans. They drank iced lager and Margie said she had been feeling so low before they came that she had been sitting here wondering how she could move the furniture round for a new image.

Arthur and Felicity groaned, and Arthur explained to David, 'She's always doing that. She's never outgrown the doll's house she had for her seventh birthday.'

'I seem to be outgrowing most else,' sighed Margie, squinting down at her straining cardigan. She went on sighing, looking at Felicity. 'How do you manage to keep the figure of a twelve-year-old?'

'Give over,' said Felicity. 'I don't look in the least like a twelve-year-old. Short of inches I might be, but not where it matters.'

'True,' said David, and anyone could see that beneath the sweater she wore was a woman, but of course Arthur and Margie hooted with laughter and decided he was speaking from closer observation.

Felicity didn't really mind. It was a long time since she had allowed herself time to let her hair down, and they were having fun. After the meal they moved furniture. Margie wanted a massive wardrobe and a chest of drawers switched in the bedroom, and when Arthur protested, 'But that was how it used to be,' she said, 'Yes, it was better that way, wasn't it?'

If David Holle hadn't turned up Arthur and Margie would have had difficulty hauling the stuff around, but with him helping Arthur it looked fairly easy and rather hilarious. They all did a lot of laughing, and while the men went to wash grimy hands Felicity and Margie refilled the wardrobe from clothes piled on the bed.

'Oh *yes*,' gurgled Margie, '*very* sexy!'

'I suppose so.' Felicity wasn't denying that. 'But you're wrong, you know, there's nothing going on.'

Margie took off her old cardigan and put on a smarter chunky rainbow-hued knitted jacket. 'You don't say,' she said to her own reflection in the mirror of the wardrobe door. 'Well, if you've only known each other since yesterday I could believe you, but he can't keep his eyes off you, even when he's moving furniture.'

'So long as it's only his eyes I don't mind,' quipped Felicity, but Margie's grin was frankly disbelieving.

The evening passed quickly. 'Anyone want the news?' Arthur asked. They were drinking a pleasant red wine, sprawled comfortably. Felicity was still on her cushion, but by now she was leaning back against the sofa and she had decided that she didn't really mind David stroking her hair. It was quite soothing.

'No, *please*!' Margie protested as Arthur switched on the television, and a politician, looking unctuous and mouthing platitudes, filled the screen. 'It'll only be depressing, it's always depressing, and just when we're so cosy.'

Arthur switched off, but for Felicity the mood had changed. For one thing she had realised that it was ten o'clock, time she was setting off for home, and the noise of the wind suddenly seemed to rise above the crackling of the logs. She said, 'We must be going,' scrambling to her feet.

'Why don't you stay the night?' Arthur suggested, and Margie chimed in, 'Yes, of course you must. There's no need to turn out in this if you don't have anybody staying. We'll open another bottle and have a fry-up.'

'Thank you,' said Felicity, 'but I really must——'

'You can have the bedroom,' offered Margie with expansive hospitality.

'Thank you, but no.' That was still Felicity, David wasn't saying anything.

'All right, then,' said Margie. 'The sofa opens up and it's comfortable.'

'I'm sure it is,' said David, and Felicity could see herself spending the night with him, because that was how they all expected it to be, unless she took a firm stand. Besides, if they did open more wine, she might forget that the attraction between herself and this man might seem passionate and real but was, in fact, pure fantasy.

She said desperately, 'I *have* to get back. I have to check that the shutters are all secured or I could have my windows smashed. Just listen to that wind!'

'Couldn't you phone the boathouse?' Margie began, but David was helping Felicity into her coat.

'Another time, then,' said Arthur.

Even in the shelter of the Yard the wind screamed at them when they opened the shop door. 'Are you sure you won't stay?' Margie was still trying to make her change her mind, but Felicity hurried off, head down, between the buildings towards the car, and the wind whooshed up the road from the sea with a battering force that nearly knocked her off her feet. She ran gasping, and when David opened the car door she almost fell in.

A moment later he was sitting beside her, closing his door, 'That was a speedy exit,' he remarked affably. 'One might almost have thought you were running away from something.'

So she had been. From the risk of sharing a room with him for the night, and he knew it. 'Don't take things so personally,' she said.

'I rarely do.' He smiled. 'Besides, how could you be running away from me when I'm still with you?'

'Exactly. So, shall we go?'

They drove down the deserted street, and the lights of the town were soon left behind, and the night was black, and Felicity found herself wishing she had stayed with Arthur and Margie, because she was becoming profoundly and progressively uneasy with this man with whom she was riding alone into the darkness.

CHAPTER FIVE

Now they were on the open road the wind buffeted the car unmercifully. Felicity was used to high winds, but this was turning into a wild night, and if she had been with anyone else she would have shown some apprehension. As it was, she held down the gasps when they emerged briefly from the shelter of the hedges, and received an almighty clout that made the car reverberate. She didn't want David Holle telling her it was going to be all right, she knew that, and even less did she need him touching her reassuringly, smiling at her.

She slithered down in her seat, hands deep in the pockets of her coat and her shoulders hunched, making herself as small as possible because she didn't want to brush against him. This was going to be a bumpy ride and she did not want to sway his way.

She was tensing up so that her throat seemed to be closing, and if she could have thought of anything worth saying her voice would have squeaked. But she couldn't think of a thing, and that didn't often happen to her.

He was silent too. It was a super car, but she had never passed a more uncomfortable journey, far worse than on the way down. The darkness inside seemed to press in on the windows, and on her until it was almost an effort to breathe.

She was glad to reach Tregorran Cove, although there was nobody about, not a living soul. She was nearly home now, and as soon as the car drew up in the boatyard she jumped out and hurried off. But he caught up with her right away, she wasn't going to lose him no matter how fast she went, and when he put an arm around her she stiffened but managed to say lightly, 'Jan was right, gale force,' as they walked on to the beach where her torch threw a pale beam.

Ahead moonlight glinted on the sea and the shining path of the causeway leading to the dark shape of Gull Rock House. 'Great-looking place you've got there,' remarked David. 'Pure Gothic.'

'Weird enough for the sea-witch?'

'Could have been built for her.'

It looked dark and empty, but Mrs Clemo would have left lights on, and fixed the shutters before she left.

Inside the house would be warm and waiting for them.

A sudden gust made Felicity lurch and her torch swing high, narrowly missing David's jaw. 'Knock me out, lady,' he said solemnly, 'and you'll never make it.'

Of course she could have walked the causeway alone, but that made her smile, and it was quite a struggle against a wind that seemed to have turned playful and boisterous, pushing them together, shoving them ahead a couple of paces and then using all its force against them, so that she was clinging to David's arm and letting him take the brunt of it. By the time they reached the steps leading up to the front door she was weak, from the buffeting and from laughter. It had been like riding a roller-coaster. She fumbled in her purse for her key while he held the torch, and when the heavy oak door opened warmth and light spilled out and Sam bounded forward barking joyfully.

'Home at last,' said David. For me, she thought, not for you; but Sam seemed as pleased to see David as Felicity and, as long as he was a paying guest, she supposed that David Holle was entitled to consider Gull Rock House a home from home.

One of the side lamps burned in this room and she looked across at her grandfather's chair, in the shadows of the fireglow, and almost believed for a moment that he was watching her. He wouldn't approve of the way she was using David Holle. He was a straightforward man who had never cheated in his life. And neither am I cheating, thought Felicity. He isn't getting what he expects, but I warned him he wouldn't. I'm playing straight with him in every way but Deirdre, and Deirdre is a debt he owes and on that I am simply squaring accounts.

She had been walking around, switching on more lights. In the kitchen she took off her coat and hung it

behind the door and looked for his. He hung it beside
hers as if he was at home in his own kitchen. If they
stayed down here he would sit in the wooden armchair,
just as he had last night, and she would rather not sit
watching him. 'My room has a fire laid,' she said. 'I'm
going to light it, I'm going up there, but if you prefer to
stay here I'll stir up this fire.'

'I prefer to be with you.'

'Fine.' He was welcome to stay with her for a while,
but if he had erotic plans for the rest of the night they
were doomed to disappointment, because he would be
off to his own bed around midnight. 'See you in a few
minutes, then,' she said.

The fire lit as soon as she put a match to it and
almost at once was burning brightly. A fire was a
comfort on a night when you could hear the wind
howling even through thick walls and shuttered
windows. Felicity remembered when storms had woken
her as a child how she had listened in the darkness and
'heard' the church bells, muffled and sweet. All fantasy,
all make-believe, but it was sad that you lost the magic
as you grew older.

Her hair was a tangled mess. If David had stayed in
the lounge she would have washed it, but as he would
be walking into this room any moment she had to settle
for a quick towelling. She was sitting in front of the fire,
hairbrush in hand, when he knocked on the door.

His hair was damp too. It looked rough and dark,
and she had a crazy urge to jump up and run to him
and run her fingers through his hair, smoothing it, then
ruffling again, smiling at him, risking what he would do
to her. She began to brush her own hair very hard.
'Come to the fire,' she invited. 'Do sit down.'

He had a sketch pad, and that was a relief, showing
he had other ideas for passing the time, apart from

seducing her. The longer she could put off that scene
the better. Still brushing her hair, she went to a little
corner cabinet and offered, 'A drink?'

'Why not? I'm driving nowhere else tonight.'

She rarely used this cabinet, but there were glasses,
and sherry and brandy, in it. If he wanted anything else
it would have to come from the bar downstairs.
'Brandy?' she suggested.

'Thank you.' He had already begun sketching and
she asked,

'Studies for the sea-witch?'

'Wait and see.' The daguerreotype was still on the
wall. He didn't turn to copy it, so either he was
sketching from memory or using Felicity as his model.
She suspected the latter, and she wasn't too happy
about that. When she sat down she rested her cheek
against the wing of her chair so that her face was half
hidden, but David didn't ask her to change her
position, so if he was making studies of her he was
doing them mostly from memory too.

It hadn't been raining when they ran over the
causeway, the air had been damp and cold, but it hadn't
been raining. It sounded as if it was now, or the gales
were driving the sea high over the rocks. You could
hear crashing waves, roaring like thunder. She winced,
and David asked, 'Do storms upset you?'

'Not unless they're very bad ones.' This one was
getting worse and she tried to shut it out, telling him, 'I
love the sound of the sea, but I come from a race of
women who feared for their men on nights like this. My
father was lost off this coast.'

'I'm sorry.'

Felicity wasn't bidding for sympathy. She was
explaining why, although she knew she was safe, a
raging sea filled her with foreboding. 'About my father?

I never knew him. It happened a few weeks before I was born.'

'And your mother?'

'When I was nine. She and my grandmother were in a car crash.'

'So all those years it was just you and your grandfather?'

She had never been lonely. She protested, 'I had lots of friends here, and during term time I was away at school.' She bit her lip at this chance to say, 'Where one of my friends was the girl you came looking for too late,' but when he asked, 'What did the Captain drink?' she'd missed the chance.

'What?'

'What was his preference? Anything in particular?'

A funny question! She said, 'Beer, I suppose, mostly. He liked the occasional rum. Why?'

'You're already specialising in local dishes, you could also offer them Captain's Punch.'

'Now that's a thought.' She sat up straighter, eyes brightening. 'I could, couldn't I? Hot and spiced on cold nights, iced in the summer. With a rum base.' She pondered, then grinned, 'How about me mixing us up a brew?'

'You're mixing your characters, it's a witch's brew.' David smiled back, and this time the smile was in his eyes too.

'Witches do love potions,' she said gaily. 'What about a liqueur mixture? Something sweet, with honey in it.' He grimaced, but the idea was a good one, she could mix her own special drinks, give them a name and some sales talk when the customers came. She offered, 'In the meantime, how about some coffee with your brandy?'

'In a while,' he said. 'Sit still for now.' He was still

sketching. 'Tell me about the sea-witch. Tell me what your grandfather used to tell you.'

Felicity looked into the fire, listening to the wind. 'Well, how she came here, in a storm.'

'On a night like this?'

'Very like this, I should think. And they said she never was on a ship, that she came from the village under the sea, bobbed up to look at the storm and got herself swept up on the beach, stark naked, where William found her. Her wrapped her in his jacket, he was a gentleman, was Willie, and carried her home.'

'Did she grow old?' He was sketching all the time.

'Not very, but my grandfather remembered that she used to soothe away aches and pains, the birds would come to her, and if she didn't like you watch out.'

She went on, telling him the old anecdotes, and he looked up at her often so that she accepted he was sketching her and waited for him to finish and show her. When he put the pad aside she held out a hand. 'Please let me see.'

She gasped when he gave it to her, because the sketch was of an old man smoking a pipe as he had been in the snapshot, but it had a depth that the photograph had missed. No doubt about David's skill as an artist, the humour and the strength and the kindness were all there, and Felicity said wonderingly, 'How could you know what he was like when you never met him?'

'I know that you loved him from the way you say his name.' Tears filled her eyes and he added quietly, 'I would like to have met him.'

'He'd have liked you,' she heard herself say, and thought, No, he wouldn't, not after the way you treated Deirdre; although every other way he would have liked you. 'May I keep this?' she asked.

'Of course.'

'How shall you paint the sea-witch?' She blinked the tears away and joked, '*Not* stark naked!'

'Not even rising from the waves like Venus?'

'Certainly not.' The lights flickered and she jerked round in alarm. 'Oh *no*, we're not going to have a power failure! I should have brought a lamp up, it's always a risk.' She was on her feet. 'It'll be all right, I've got lots of oil lamps and stacks of candles.'

'Can I help?' David offered, and she said, 'Be right back with a couple of oil lamps.'

The clamour of the wind seemed louder out here in the corridor, and if they were plunged into darkness before she'd organised the alternate lighting it would be awkward. Felicity ran downstairs, Sam close behind her. 'Just listen to that!' she gasped. 'It's a long time since we had a battering like this. In the morning Mrs Clemo will be saying it's Great-great-grandmamma's storm and we should have left her well alone.'

She wasn't sure that was funny. She lit an oil lamp and set it on the kitchen table, put matches, two electric torches and another oil lamp on a tray to carry upstairs, then went back into the lounge and built the fire high.

She shivered suddenly, wondering if long ago, in those houses under the sea, women had built up fires and listened to the storm before the waves came over them. She was getting morbid. It was all this talk of sea-witches, and that was a nonsense, because her great-great-grandmother had been Carlotta Lopez, sailing with her father, captain of the *Santa Monica*, the ship that was wrecked. And every year gales lashed this coast, tonight was no worse than other nights had been.

Felicity could see nothing through the windows unless she opened them and swung back the shutters, so she went to the front door. As soon as she unlocked that Sam trotted out on to the top step, his evening constitutional consisted of an amble over the rocks and the immediate beach, but he wasn't going far tonight. The sea was almost up to their door, there was no sign of the causeway, and Felicity stood transfixed at the awesome sight of black churning water lashed by the winds.

One wave, overtopping the rest, came without warning, smooth and shining and high as the sky, and if David had not dragged her back it would have sucked her under. As it was she fell sprawling, drenched to the skin, as the wave broke against the open door, losing its power but flooding in. David flung himself against the door, slamming it to, and she starting screaming.

She was fighting him, as desperately as though she fought the sea, and the element of surprise when she leapt at him almost had him off balance. She hit and clawed, shrieking, 'Open the door, you fool, Sam's out there!' until he literally threw her back and roared, 'The dog's behind you!'

Sam, less of a fool than she, had backed off instead of stopping to stare. She got to her knees, looking half drowned and feeling punch drunk. David, pretty wet himself, was glaring at her and she muttered, 'Sorry, I didn't see him. That wasn't very clever.'

'That's an understatement,' he retorted with withering scorn. 'Personally I'd rate it as criminal daftness. Can I take one of these?' He nodded towards the tray with the lamps, picked up an electric torch and went upstairs, and Felicity got up off her knees to mop the flagstones and drape a rug that had been soaked over a stool near the fire.

It was unnerving, thinking of the sea beating on the door, but this side of the house doors and windows should hold. This was the sheltered side. Lord save us from the open sea, she prayed. 'And you come upstairs, you stupid dog,' she said to Sam, back on the hearthrug. And then, 'Yes, all right, I know, you're smarter than I am.'

She left a lamp burning in the Captain's Room, took dry clothes into a bathroom, changed out of her sodden ones, and sat on the side of the bath paddling her feet in hot water. She would have liked to get into the bath, but the lights were flickering and she felt safer with clothes on.

It was lucky for her that David had followed her downstairs. If that wave had swept her out she might not have got back, the currents would be crazy out there right now. She would have to say thank you for that, and she couldn't tell him she had saved Deirdre, and Deirdre had jumped in, and how was that for daftness?

It had shaken her. All of her felt cold except her feet and she couldn't sit here much longer, but she pulled out the plug reluctantly and waited until the last of the bath water had swirled away before she dabbed her feet dry.

She hoped David hadn't gone to his room. He probably had because he'd need to change too, but she hoped he wasn't staying there, because if she knocked on that door it could give the wrong impression. He was finding her less fanciable than he had earlier, her hysterics had put him off, but all the same she would prefer to find him out of his bedroom.

The lights went out and although she was expecting that, and she had a torch within reach, it was another shock. She swore on a long-drawn-out sigh, switched on the torch, and went back to her room.

The fire was in here, the lamp was burning, and David was waiting. He was sitting by the fire, he'd changed slacks and sweater, and he said as Felicity walked in, 'I was beginning to wonder whether I ought to come looking for you again.'

'I was in the bath.'

'Haven't you had enough water for one night?'

'This was hot.' She gulped. 'Thank goodness you did come looking. You do have splendid timing.'

'Why the hell did you open that door?' He still looked grim and sounded disgruntled.

'I wanted to see,' she said. 'I thought, it can't be as bad as it sounds, but it was.'

'The story of my life.' Felicity was surprised how relieved she was when he laughed and how the darkness and danger seemed to recede. This house was rock and tomorrow the lights would go on, and she began to smile too, walking towards the fire and the man who sat there with the dog at his feet.

She stopped suddenly, clapped a hand to her mouth and took it away to ask, 'Have you looked in a mirror lately?'

'Not since I shaved this morning—why?'

'I think,' she took another step, peering into his face, 'well, I think I might have blacked your eye.'

He touched his cheekbone. 'That doesn't surprise me. Do you do much all-in wrestling?' Even in the diffused lamplight there was a puffiness.

'I'm so sorry. I lost my head.' She was ashamed of that. She sat down, confused and contrite. 'And I don't do much panicking, I promise you. What I think it was was talking about the houses under the sea, and then when I opened the door and that great wave reared up,' she gestured height and horror, 'I thought it had come to get us. I was paralysed. I'd have been swept off that step all right, so thank you, very much, for being around.'

David reached and took her hand, and her fingers closed over his instinctively, as though she had done this a hundred times. 'Nothing will get you while I'm around,' he said, and Felicity believed him and said, 'I know.'

'Would you have jumped into the sea after a dog?' He was studying her face carefully and she answered honestly,

'For Sam, yes,' and wrinkled her nose trying to make it sound less dramatic. 'But you know me, a bit on the daft side, I'd jump in after anybody.' She thought of Deirdre again, then David's hold tightened into a grip that hurt and drove all other thoughts from her mind.

'Kick the habit,' he said, 'I need you alive,' and she said lightly, 'Oh, I do too.'

'I'm serious.' He looked so deep into her eyes that her head jerked back. He spoke so quietly that the noise of the wind should have drowned his words, but she heard every one. He said, 'I feel like William must have felt when he found his sea-witch, because I've been searching for you on a lot of beaches, and in a lot of towns and countries, for a long time.'

It was a pretty speech. Had he used something like that for Deirdre? But when she looked into his eyes a hunger seized her that she had never known before, for the roughness of his hair and the hard familiar feel of his body.

She closed her eyes tight, shutting him out but still breathing in a man smell, clean and sharp, that made her head spin. She said, 'I don't know. Please don't rush me. I don't know.' And she was not pretending, she was in desperate confusion.

David loosed her hand and sat back in his chair. She still had her eyes shut, but she knew that. 'That's all right,' he said. 'I do, and one of us knowing is a good start.'

She looked up cautiously and he went on, 'So let's

talk about making this place of yours a commercial success. Will you let me back you beyond the publicity?'

'I don't know.' That seemed to be all she could say. She began to pace the room, stopping at the globe and spinning it slowly like a worry bead. When she was in control of herself again she asked, 'How do you mean, back me?'

'With an interest-free loan for whatever you need.'

Who could turn down an offer like that? Who had ever heard of an offer like that? 'You're offering a lot,' she commented.

'No more than I can deliver.'

She had no right to let him make these kind of promises. 'And anything I need you can deliver?' She smiled to lighten a situation that was getting out of hand.

'Try me.' He was meaning more than money, he was meaning other needs, and there was an undeniable stirring in her flesh when she looked at him that she must guard against. 'He made himself my life,' Deirdre had said, and nothing like that was going to happen to Felicity, but tonight's gales could be causing havoc and she wasn't that well insured. If the bank wouldn't advance her any more she might need a loan. If she did she would insist on paying reasonable interest.

'Tomorrow,' she said. 'Let's leave it till tomorrow. By then you may have second thoughts.'

'Not about anything to do with you.' David sounded so confident that her face flamed. Before she borrowed from him she must tell him about Deirdre, and after that of course he would have second thoughts. Now she asked, 'Are you hungry?'

'Starving!'

'I'm talking about supper.' Her lips twitched, but the smile was wry. 'Like bread and cheese, because I daren't open the freezer.' If the power was off for any length of time everything refrigerated would spoil. 'And the cooker won't work. And if the water has got in downstairs it could be very soppy bread.'

'How about making a meal of each other?' He grinned at her lasciviously and Felicity knew he was doing it because he knew she was worried. She pulled a face. 'You could be too tough for me, I'll stay with bread and cheese.'

'I offer her a feast,' he announced sorrowfully, 'and she stays with bread and cheese!'

She opened her eyes wide. 'You guarantee it would be a feast?'

'Absolutely. No? Very well, you make up the fire and I'll fetch the supper.'

David picked up an electric torch and she went towards the door. 'You think the sea might have come in, don't you?' said Felicity, 'and I might go hysterical on you again.'

'Nothing of the sort.'

'It might,' she said, 'but I wouldn't.'

They went together, and she held her breath until they rounded the corner of the corridor and saw the glow of the fire from the lounge. The lamp was still burning in the kitchen and all the windows and doors stood firm.

Felicity gave a gasp of relief, then pretended she hadn't been scared. 'Have you noticed how thick the doors are? And the shutters? This house has been here for well over two hundred years.' She began to fill a tray, getting food out of the fridge fast: chicken, sausages, cheese, pâté. Outside the sea was still pounding, but this time she was opening no doors for it. She said, 'I suppose it could be breaking over us. Maybe we're one of the houses under the water.'

That was an obvious impossibility, she was chattering from nerves, and when David took her in his arms she stood on tiptoe and pressed her face against his. 'You're too warm for a mermaid,' he said.

'Suppose we're under the sea. Suppose we never get out. What shall we do, just the two of us for ever?'

It was banter now, like lovers' talk, and like a lover he said, 'Just the two of us could pass the time very pleasurably,' and a little shiver of delight ran through her.

Then she stepped away. 'Would you get a bottle of wine from the rack behind the bar, please? Pick what you like, on the house. I'll bring the food.'

She didn't want to linger; it was cosier in the smaller room. She hurried upstairs and they placed the tray on a little round table in front of the fire, and Sam sat up, tail wagging and glistening eyes on the chicken. 'Fair shares,' Felicity assured him, pulling it apart.

The storm raged on, but they ate and talked, and David made her laugh, and kept her fascinated by telling her about places he had been and people he had met. She knew he was doing this to stop her listening to the wind and that was kind. Deirdre had said he was kind until he tired of her, but tonight Felicity was too weary to bother about moral judgments. After a couple of glasses of wine David's past didn't seem to matter, and right now he seemed the right man to have around.

Long after the meal was finished, when Felicity was explaining what stargazy pie was, a yawn took over half way through a sentence that she changed to, 'I'm shattered, I'll have to get to bed.'

'Do you want me to go?'

She looked across in the lamplight, at the firm contours of his mouth and chin, and she wanted to say,

'Stay with me and hold me close.' She rubbed her eyes, trying to keep them clear and clear her head too, because she must not say that. 'It is only our second night,' she prevaricated.

'So it is. Hard to believe.'

It *was* hard to believe, and not just because of what Deirdre had told her but because she had done her own discovering. She could still hear the wind screaming. It was going to be a night of storm and the house would be dark and it would be sensible to stay together. She asked, 'Is it going to be the way I want?'

'Of course.'

'Then I would like you to stay in this room, but I would like to sleep over there and I would like you to sleep in a chair.' She drew a deep breath, 'Or I'll take the chair and you can have the divan.'

'The chair will do for me,' he said, and Felicity got up and told herself she was glad he didn't kiss her goodnight, nor even touch her when she passed him. She said, 'Thank you,' and went to the divan that opened into a bed. She didn't open it tonight, nor bring out the bedclothes except for one pillow from the drawer underneath. She didn't undress, except for kicking off her shoes, and when she curled up, head on the pillow, drowsiness settled over her like a warm duvet.

A few minutes later David turned out the lamp so that there was only the fireglow. She could still see him dimly in profile, and she called softly, 'David.'

'Yes?'

'How will you explain your black eye in the morning? Will you tell them I slugged you?'

'I shall say I bumped into something in the dark.' She knew he was smiling, and so did she.

'I'm sorry,' she said. 'Does it hurt?'

'No.'

'I'm glad. Is that chair all right?'

'Adequate.'

'Does adequate mean all right?'

After a moment or two he asked, 'Am I being obtuse? Have you changed your mind?'

'About what?'

'If you don't want me to join you be quiet and go to sleep.'

Felicity raised herself on an elbow. 'There's no reason why you shouldn't lie down,' she said. 'This divan makes a double bed. I'd rather not be on my own, but I don't want you to spend an uncomfortable night. Suppose we each keep to our own half?'

'Suppose you stop talking rubbish?' He turned to look across at her but, with the firelight behind him, she couldn't make out his expression. 'There is no way I could lie beside you all night and not make love to you, and you've got to know that. So do you want me to stay over here or not?'

'Over there!' her voice rose shrilly.

'Right,' he said. 'Goodnight.'

After that she was quiet as a mouse. She didn't think she talked in her sleep. If she did it wouldn't be her fault, and calling out in a dream surely wouldn't count. She lay very still, listening to the storm and another sound—not the church bells under the sea but the hard thudding of her own heart—until at long last she fell asleep.

CHAPTER SIX

THE knock on the door and Mrs Clemo calling, 'Are you there?' woke Felicity. Before she had time to move, much less reply, Mrs Clemo had walked in. 'Good lord, what time is it?' Felicity gasped.

Mrs Clemo did a double-take, from a tousle-haired Felicity on the divan, with rumpled pillow and a rug that David must have put over her some time during the night without disturbing her, to David sitting at the desk that used to be the Captain's.

'Half past eight,' said David.

'*Never!* But I always wake before seven. I suppose it was because I didn't get to sleep till late. Gosh, what a night!' If Felicity had been left alone she could well have slept on, she was so muzzy that she hardly knew what she was saying, but she could see that David was having difficulty keeping a straight face and Mrs Clemo was looking shocked, and then she croaked, 'The storm, I mean.'

Mrs Clemo said nothing, but her lips tightened as if there was plenty she could say, and Felicity stood up and hoped it was being noted that she was fully clad. When she got Mrs Clemo alone she would explain what had happened, but she didn't want any kind of scene in front of David.

'Seems to have blown over,' she said chattily. The shutters had been swung back and the skies were grey, but the wind had dropped. 'How's the eye?' she enquired. It hadn't gone black and the swelling had subsided. 'Not too bad,' she decided, and smiled, 'Sorry all the same.'

'You don't look too bad yourself,' said David solemnly. 'Everything considered.' Felicity heard Mrs Clemo's sniff and tried to push her hair tidy, muttering, 'I must do something about my hair, I must look a fright. What are you doing?'

'Making a few notes.' So he was, and he had a mug of tea or coffee, so he had been up and about, going down to the kitchen, covering her with a rug while she slept. He went on, 'You'll need some brochures, and when the season starts again throw a first-night party with some celebrity names. I'll gather them in for you.'

That would get into the local papers at least, perhaps even a mention in the nationals. That would be lovely publicity. 'Lovely,' she said. 'Who could you get?'

Mrs Clemo cleared her throat and announced, 'We brought the letters. There's one from that girl you used to go to school with, what's her name?'

Her name was Deirdre, of course. Emphatically Mrs Clemo did not approve of what seemed to be going on and she was all set to blow it. 'That's nice,' Felicity babbled, and tried frantically to change the subject. 'I don't think I can remember a worse storm. Can you? I mean, the water's come up often enough before, but last night—the *waves*! What was it like on the sea-front?'

Mrs Clemo took her time replying then said ominously, 'Haven't you been down? No, of course you haven't. Well, it was before the war that this happened before.'

Felicity felt hollow. Something was wrong, maybe in the house, and Mrs Clemo thought Felicity should have been up and doing not out for the count after a night of dalliance. She didn't stop for questions. She ran, expecting some appalling damage when she looked down the stairs. But everything seemed just as she had seen it last, except that now it was daylight and Jessie was coming through the door from the dining room. 'What a terrible night,' said Jessie.

David had been down here. If the sea had come in he wouldn't have calmly made himself coffee and gone back upstairs to jot down a few notes. Felicity looked around her. 'What's happened? Your mother's just frightened me silly! I don't know what I expected to find, but everything looks all right.'

'It's outside.' Jessie jerked her head at the door and Felicity went apprehensively towards it. The water wouldn't be coming in this time, but her hands were shaking as she lifted the heavy latch. She was aware of David behind her and without turning she said, 'Get ready to grab me again if there's a freak wave waiting.'

It was quiet and calm this morning, everything seemed washed to a uniform grey, but evidence of last night's storm stretched ahead of her. The causeway was no longer recognisable as a path. Stones had been dislodged, upturned, swept away. She could see breaks in the harbour wall where the sea had breached it and as she stood, shocked speechless, Jessie said, 'Well, we got here.'

And no mean feat, Mrs Clemo at her age scrambling over that rocky obstacle course. Felicity felt a warm rush of affection. 'Oh, Jessie, you're wonderful, both of you. How did you get your mother over that?'

'You'd be surprised,' said Jessie. 'She wasn't being left behind. We didn't know what might have happened to you out here.'

Mrs Clemo thinks she knows now, thought Felicity, and Jessie thinks she's got a pretty good idea too. She said, 'Your mother's told you about David?'

'Pleased to meet you,' Jessie sounded as though she was reserving judgment, and Felicity turned back to the causeway remarking ruefully, 'That's going to put the customers off.'

'Oh, I don't know,' said David. 'We could offer mountaineering in the brochure.'

'It's not funny,' snapped Felicity. It could have been a tragedy, but it wasn't, because he had said 'we', which meant he considered it his problem too. 'Have you had second thoughts on last night's offer of a loan?' she asked, and knew that Jessie was listening, fascinated.

'None,' said David.

'It still holds?'

'Whatever you need.'

This morning she had no choice, and of course she would pay him back. Right now she had to say, 'It seems to be out of my hands. As you can see, I can use some help.'

'I'll get it done,' he said. 'And the power failure, were you cut off too?' He was asking Jessie who said all Tregorran Cove was and there'd been flooding in some of the houses on the sea-front. Not her mother's, though—Jessie's home was halfway up the hill—and the cars in the boatyard were all right and the phones were still working.

'I'll get over there.' David went towards the kitchen and his mac hanging behind the kitchen door, and Felicity hurried after him, remembering that Deirdre's letter would probably be lying on the table. She couldn't go into all that today. First things first.

She spotted the French stamps as she went through the door and gathered up the three letters and a circular, took them to the dresser and opened the envelope with the Queen's head on it and Edward Cunliffe's writing. David got into his mac and watched her. She had her back to him, Deirdre's letter on the dresser covered by the circular and an official-looking buff envelope, but she got this prickling in the nape of her neck.

'Everything all right?' he asked.

'Sure. Why not?' She turned, smiling.

'Mrs Clemo sounded as though this morning's mail was on a par with last night's weather.'

'Well, there's the water rate, that's adding insult to injury. And a letter from a girl friend, and there's this,' she waved the page she had been reading, 'from the man I was telling you about, who's stayed twice and wants to book for a weekend next month.'

'I'll look forward to meeting him,' said David.

'Nice little chap,' said Jessie who had followed them in. 'She says it's her cooking, but we think he's fallen for her.'

'Him I will meet,' said David. 'By the way, if you want a cup of coffee there's a flask by the desk. I boiled the water over the fire.'

'My goodness, aren't you adaptable?' Felicity's voice was showing the strain of all this deception, and he put his arms around her and the tension ebbed away. 'Don't worry,' he said. 'Everything will be all right.' He kissed her cheek, gently, but it felt such an intimate touch that it seemed they were alone, and then he left her, back to the dresser, facing a wide-eyed Jessie.

When the kitchen door closed behind David Felicity said, 'And what would you have done? You know we've been struggling along hand to mouth and I've got no spare cash, and as well as money he's got famous friends. He says he'll bring some of them, that should get us talked about so folk know we're here.'

'There's a letter there from one of his friends,' said Jessie drily, and Felicity snapped,

'Well, I haven't told him how well I knew Deirdre— and what's that got to do with it? He's really interested in this place, he thinks it's got great potential.'

'Oh yes?' said Jessie derisively, 'Like that one's interested in your cooking.' Felicity was still holding Edward Cunliffe's letter, and she pointed out, .

'If we'd dished up duff food for Mr Cunliffe that first night he wouldn't have stayed on nor come back,' and Jessie, who agreed but wasn't interested in Edward Cunliffe, enquired sweetly,

'And what did we dish up for Mr Holle last night, then?'

Before Felicity could reply Mrs Clemo strode into the kitchen, snapped, 'No beds to make this morning,' and marched over to the sink, her spine rigid with disapproval.

'She means David's bed wasn't slept in,' Felicity said wearily, 'But believe it or not, that doesn't answer your question.' She had to raise her voice over the noise of Mrs Clemo clattering pans. 'We ate supper together in my room and sat talking most of the night because I'd had a scare. I was nearly swept off the steps out there and David pulled me back, and the electricity was off and it was pretty grim, so I was very glad of his company. But he slept in a chair and I slept on the divan and all I took off were my shoes. Satisfied?'

'Wasn't there a letter from Deirdre?' asked Mrs Clemo, who had seen the name and address written on the back. 'Are you going to tell her her young man's moved in here?' and Felicity's patience short-circuited in a flash of irritation so that she almost yelled,

'All right! I should have told him Deirdre and I were old mates and she never stopped talking about him. I should have done and I didn't, and it was stupid and I wish I had, and I will. But all I care about this morning is getting that causeway repaired, and any man who promises me everything is going to be all right on a morning like this is somebody I can't afford to lose.'

She stopped for breath, biting her lip, astounded to find herself almost weeping, 'Oh, can't you both *see*, we *need* him?'

There was silence for a few seconds, then Mrs Clemo said, 'I saw him go, and Sam. What's he going to do about the causeway?'

'Get it fixed, somehow, I think.'

'Be a good job done,' said Mrs Clemo. 'What was wrong with his eye? Why were you apologising for it?'

'I didn't have to fight him off either,' said Felicity, 'but when he pulled me back last night I sort of hit him. I panicked because I thought Sam was in the sea, only David knew he wasn't.'

'It's a marvel how the Captain's dog's taken to him,' said Mrs Clemo.

'A man can change his mind, I should hope,' said Jessie. 'They weren't married, were they?'

'No.' Felicity tore open Deirdre's letter, hoping desperately that Deirdre was still in the same frame of mind as when she'd said goodbye. Optimistic, quite happy, never wanting to hear David's name again. As she read she smiled, because this was all great news. In middle age Deirdre's mother seemed to be enjoying having a daughter whom everyone took for her sister, and was anxious for Deirdre to stay as long as she liked. Deirdre sounded quite ecstatic about her new life, making friends, meeting dishy men.

'She doesn't even mention David,' said Felicity. 'She's having a fantastic time, and before she went she told me to tear up any letters if he wrote here, and she left his photograph and told me to throw that away.' It *was* over.

'So what's the fuss about?' Jessie was coming round to the opinion that David Holle could be just what the guest-house needed, and Mrs Clemo agreed that after last night's storm it sounded that way. Although she still had misgivings, and she hoped that when the reckoning came Felicity wouldn't be wishing she had never invited Deirdre Osborne down here and never set eyes on David Holle . . .

'Funny about the storm, wasn't it?' said Jessie. 'You having a painting done of her, calling her up like, and then the storm coming.'

They had left Mrs Clemo downstairs when Felicity asked Jessie, 'Would you give me a hand in the attic? I'm looking for old letters and papers, anything going back a hundred years or so.'

The junk of generations was stock-piled under the eaves of Gull Rock House, and the two girls poked gingerly around by the light of a ship's lamp hung on a rafter. The furniture up there was mostly broken: three-legged chairs, cracked mirrors and pictures, a lurching tallboy with half its drawers missing. 'Not many handymen in my family,' Felicity remarked to Jessie. 'I suppose all this was put away because somebody thought it would get repaired one day, only it never did.'

She had come up here before she opened her guest-house but found little of use and nothing of value. Today it was the old cases and trunks that concerned her, and they ranged from the cabin trunk that had gone backwards and forwards with her own belongings and hadn't seen the light of day since she left school, to a battered old tin trunk, well back from the trapdoor and covered in dust, that looked ancient and promising.

When they reached it, not having had much success up till then, Felicity said, 'Here's our last hope,' and Jessie shuddered, 'It could have anything in it. Have you ever opened it?'

'I've opened everything in my time,' said Felicity. 'That one is books and papers, I looked in there years ago, but it's never been sorted.' She found her old hockey stick and scooped away the festoons of dusty webs, wishing she had suggested that David might come up here, preferably alone. Jess, with the same idea, offered her husband's help, 'Jan would get this down for us,' as Felicity knocked up the catch and lifted the lid on the end of her stick, keeping well back.

But with the lid open they both took a step forward and peered in, and here was probably the result of a long-ago turn-out, with everything being dropped into the tin trunk and dumped in the attic. 'Some of it might have something to do with Carlotta,' said Felicity, while Jessie eyed the yellowing papers in the dark trunk, waiting for the spiders to crawl out.

'Funny about the storm, wasn't it?' said Jessie suddenly. She was less superstitious than her mother, but last night's gales had been exceptional.

'Nothing weird about it,' said Felicity, cautiously lifting the edges of some papers and trying to read what they were without actually removing any. 'That storm had been building up all week, and my great-great-grandmother was no more a witch than yours was.'

'That's not what my mother says,' Jessie grinned.

'Felicity, Jessie!' Mrs Clemo was calling them from the bottom of the ladder. 'Felicity, you've got a visitor.'

'Who?' Felicity went to look down and Gordon was looking up with David behind him. 'We met in the car park,' David explained cheerfully.

'I came out to see if you were all right,' said Gordon. 'I rang the boathouse and all they could tell me was that there'd been some damage done. Nobody seemed to know how much.'

'Oh, that *was* nice of you.' Felicity felt the same

warmth for him that she had for Jessie and Mrs Clemo, struggling out here to make sure she was safe. They were her very good friends and she hoped that David had said nothing to upset Gordon. She scrambled down the ladder and she had every intention of kissing Gordon, but when she reached him something stopped her. Gordon perhaps, there was a definite constraint about him. But then there always was when anyone else was around, he always worried what other people were thinking; and maybe David was inhibiting her, standing there, watching her. It *was* David, she decided, and she did kiss Gordon, soundly, and said, 'Bless you, it's lovely to see you. It was a beastly night, wasn't it?'

'I was afraid you might be on your own,' said Gordon. 'I was worried about you,' and she felt guilty about Gordon, lying listening to the storm and worrying about Gull Rock House with the sea all around it, and Felicity maybe all on her own. She also felt guilty about the kiss, because it brought back the memory of the way David's kiss sent shock waves through her. Gordon did not. Even if he had grabbed and kissed her back passionately it would have surprised her, in front of them all, but it wouldn't have stirred her like the brush of David's lips against her cheek.

She rushed into talk and action. 'Jessie and I have been rooting through the attic and we've found an old trunk, full of papers and books. We didn't feel much like emptying it up there, it's been there so long there have to be spiders and there could be mice, and now I've got two able-bodied men here at the same time I wonder if you'd help us to shift it, because if we could get it down that would be marvellous.'

'Yes, of course,' said Gordon rather coolly.

'After a wardrobe,' said David, 'a trunk should

present no problem.' He smiled and Felicity laughed, 'Oh yes.' Margie's wardrobe, but if she mentioned that she would have to explain to Gordon why she had gone into Fenmouth yesterday afternoon and not called to see him, and she thought that thought could be in David's mind. 'Come on up,' she invited, 'and try it for weight.'

It was heavy, but they dragged and shoved it to the trapdoor, and between them got it down the ladder and into the Captain's Room, where Gordon collapsed into a chair with a deep sigh and Felicity asked anxiously, 'Are you all right? It isn't your back?' She remembered now that he had had trouble with his back once before, when she first knew him.

'No, no.' He sat bolt upright to prove it. 'I'm all right.'

'I don't think, do I?' She was stricken with remorse. 'I do impose, that's the word. Getting you all hauling filthy old tin trunks that weigh a ton!' She knew that Gordon was annoyed about it, although David chuckled, 'But you impose so seductively.'

'Anyhow,' she said, 'thank you all.' It certainly hadn't hurt David, nor Felicity herself and Jessie had only carried the lamp, but of course Gordon did have his back and it would be dreadful if he'd pulled or slipped something. She explained to him, 'We're going in for a new image, that's why I wanted to see what was in here. Well, it's an old image really,' and she talked on while David began to empty the trunk, joined after a while by Jessie.

When Felicity paused Gordon said, puzzled, 'You mean turn the house into a museum?'

'*No*, still a guest-house, just with more character.'

'You *are* desperate!' He said that with irritating smugness. 'What you'll need to do for a start,' he advised her, 'is something about the causeway, and that's going to cost you.'

She looked towards David, who was reading the front page of a brown-edged newspaper. 'The Titanic sank,' said David. 'Repairs on the causeway start this afternoon.'

'I'm sorry about the Titanic,' Felicity gurgled, 'but the news about the causeway gives me hope.' Gordon got up, so his back was all right, and said, 'I might as well be going, you seem to be coping.'

'I'll walk with you to the car,' Felicity offered.

It wasn't a walk so much as a scramble. Some of the reared-up rocks had to be climbed over, and where the pathway had been forced apart you had to jump the gaps. It looked a route for the young and agile, but Mrs Clemo had managed it, and now that David had promised help was at hand Felicity found it quite an exhilarating exercise. She had climbed cliffs and picked her way over rocks all her life, but Gordon had not, so he was not enjoying himself. He advanced with a trepidation that slowed Felicity down, because it seemed tactless to be hopping around him like a mountain goat.

Until they reached the shingle on the beach not a lot was said. Felicity did say, 'Oh dear!' when he slipped and sat, getting up with a stain of seaweed on his fawn-coloured coat. Going into the attic hadn't done the coat much good either, but she didn't mention the black marks on the sleeve, nor the seaweed, because he was annoyed about falling down and she couldn't see that information cheering him up.

Stepping off the causeway, she said, 'I do appreciate you coming to see if I was all right, and battling your way over all this.'

'The radio said it had centred over Tregorran Cove

and done some damage.' Gordon straightened his tie and his shoulders, getting his dignity back, and Felicity found that touching. She linked her hand through his arm and fell into step beside him. 'It was wild,' she said, 'but Mrs Clemo says it's fifty years since the causeway got cracked up before, so if the repairs last another half century——'

'Who is he?' asked Gordon, and she stopped and blinked.

'Do you mean——?' She looked back at the house. 'David Holle? Didn't you introduce yourselves? You came in together and you met in the car park, didn't you? Didn't you get his name?'

'I saw Sam with him,' said Gordon. 'He said he was staying at your place, he thought he recognised me from my photograph on your desk. He said you were all right and the only damage done to the house was this. He was just going back, he said.'

There were people on the sea-front, examining the wall, discussing the storm. Felicity assured several of them that Gull Rock House had escaped, and went on with Gordon into the boatyard car park. 'Has he got anything to do with this nonsense about a new image?' asked Gordon. 'I noticed he was going through that trunk without a by-your-leave.'

He was a good sort, was Gordon, and he had a right to know what was going on. 'It was his idea,' said Felicity.

'How long has he been here? How long is he staying? What's it got to do with him?' Gordon was firing staccato questions at her, and she told him,

'He's a friend of a girl who used to go to school with me. She's with her mother in the south of France now—it's all right for some—but she had a holiday here before she went. He came down a couple of days ago, thinking she was still here, and he suggested putting the old family photographs around.'

She would have to tell David about Deirdre now. Gordon's face had cleared slightly, at the mention of another girl, but not entirely. As he got into his car he said, 'Running a guest-house was a stupid idea from the start, and turning it into a peepshow isn't going to do any good. You're simply wasting your time, and I hope you're not wasting any money.'

You wouldn't give me an encouraging word to save my life, would you? she thought. You came out here because you were worried about me, but you would rather the storm had wrecked any chance of me staying in my home. You want me back in the galleries, and maybe full time in your life, and you don't give a damn what I want. 'It won't be wasted,' she said through the car window, to Gordon behind the wheel. 'The time or the money.'

She went straight back, almost running over the shingle to the causeway and hurrying, surefooted, towards the house. Nothing would be wasted. She needed David's advice and his enthusiasm, as much as his time and money, but if it took her heart's blood she would give him a solid and lasting success to show for it all.

'They're still going through that filthy old trunk,' Mrs Clemo grumbled when Felicity walked into the hall. 'I don't know why you had to get that down. You could have done yourself a mischief, mauling a thing like that.'

'Not to worry,' said Felicity. 'No casualties except for Gordon's coat, and he's just landed on a patch of seaweed, so a bit of dust hardly counts.' She ran up the stairs, her spirits soaring, feeling so lucky that she would not have been surprised if they had uncovered

Carlotta's notebook, full of secret recipes, or a purse of gold.

'I'm back,' she announced, and David straightened from the trunk, which was almost empty, while Jessie looked up from a book she was leafing through.

'How's Gordon's back?' asked David.

Felicity looked solemn. 'He didn't mention it again.'

'Does he have much trouble with it?'

'No.' She put on a face of injured innocence. 'And don't look at me like that—it's never been my fault, except today nearly. When I first went to work at the Galleries he put it out and had to go to an osteopath. If I remember rightly he was getting something off a pedestal.'

'Uh-huh,' said David.

'Not me—a bronze horse. Nobody ever put me on a pedestal.'

'You astound me.' He burst out laughing and Felicity and Jessie joined in, and Felicity thought, I'll always be able to make him smile, and it was a good feeling. She looked at the contents of the trunk, arranged fairly neatly around it, and enquired, 'Did we find anything?'

'We left the letters,' Jessie explained. 'We thought you should be the first to look at those yourself—you know, family, private like. But this is nice, isn't it?' She opened a scrapbook filled with roses and cherubs, and apple-faced golden-haired children. Pure Victorian. 'Mabel Mayne, aged eight,' was printed on the flyleaf in a round childish hand, and Felicity said, 'She was one of Carlotta's daughters. Some of these pages could be framed, couldn't they? They'd look colourful and pretty, like samplers. I know somebody who does framing.'

She set the scrapbook aside. 'David, I was thinking on the way back, while I was hopping over the rocks, how I could make the rooms look prettier, and I've always liked patchwork quilts. I've got candlewick now, they're cheaper, but there's a girl who does patchwork, quite reasonably, at another of the shops in Trevarrow's Yard. Could I get an estimate?'

She was aware of Jessie frowning. 'Whatever you want,' said David. Jessie's resemblance to her mother was very marked at the moment. She thinks I'm being greedy, thought Felicity, but it wouldn't be that much, and it's off-season so Annabel could use the money, and they would make all the difference to the bedrooms. She said, 'I'd get special terms.'

The lights came on, startling them with sudden brightness. The fault had been repaired, and that was such a relief, because there had been power failures down here that had lasted for days. 'Fantastic!' Felicity beamed at David, who said, 'That I didn't do.'

'I reckon you did,' she joked, and he said quietly,

'You are the one who turns on the lights.' She felt herself blushing, feeling awkward, although usually she could take a compliment gracefully. 'How about breakfast?' she suggested. 'Give us five minutes.'

She went out of the room with Jessie, and walking along the corridor Jessie said, 'He's mad about you.'

'Is he?' It was flattering as well as useful, this instant rapport that must wane before long.

'While you were gone,' said Jessie, 'he kept talking about you, asking me about you.'

'What did you say?' Apprehension quickened Felicity's voice, but Jessie said,

'It's all right, I didn't tell him anything about Deirdre.'

'I will,' Felicity vowed. 'Only I've got to wait for the right moment.' Which must be before Gordon met David again, and asked about the girl who was David's friend and had gone to school with Felicity.

'You don't think you're taking too much from him?' Jessie didn't want to offend Felicity, who was usually the soul of generosity and independence so that this seemed out of character. 'I mean, do we really need extras like new quilts? Are you letting him pay for them?'

Felicity shrugged, 'Why not? I'll pay him back, of course. He'll be getting a share in the profits, so it's in his interests that the bedrooms look as attractive as possible.'

'Talking of bedrooms,' drawled Jessie, 'it's more than a share in the profits he wants,' and Felicity announced, with an airy confidence that was not entirely genuine,

'I can handle men.'

'You can handle Gordon and that Mr Cunliffe,' said Jessie drily, 'but you're not going to keep that one upstairs at arms' length for long.'

Felicity realised how hungry she was when the aroma of sizzling bacon rose from the grill, and Jessie, who had left home this morning on cornflakes and bread and butter, was also inhaling blissfully. Felicity added more bacon, and another egg in the pan, and Jessie laid the table for two. David's table was already prepared in the dining room and when he came into the kitchen Felicity said, 'I'll bring yours out.'

'Out where?'

'To your table.'

'I'll join you,' he said. 'If we can sleep together we can eat together.'

'Will you *stop* it? I've only just managed to convince Mrs Clemo that you slept in the chair.' Thank goodness Mrs Clemo was not within earshot. 'And now you're giving Jessie ideas.'

Jessie laid another place at the kitchen table and

didn't say a word. She knew that David Holle wouldn't be joking like this if he and Felicity really had slept together last night. But she'd bet that tonight would be different, and neither of them would joke about that tomorrow.

She went home after breakfast. She had enjoyed her meal, and not just because she was hungry but because of the company. She always liked being with Felicity, but this morning Felicity had an extra sparkle, and David Holle was one in a million. A rich and successful man who didn't talk down and wasn't full of himself, and didn't make Jessie feel that she was in the way, sitting there with them, although you would have had to be blind and deaf not to sense something between him and Felicity that almost make the air around them crackle.

Felicity went back to the trunk and David went with her. She sat on her heels in front of a pile of letters, and he sat in the chair behind the desk, and this time he was making sketches for the sea-witch. He took the picture of Carlotta off the wall and propped it up against Gordon's photograph so that Gordon appeared to be squinting over the top.

He was sketching on typing paper and Felicity, having provided the paper, had tried to hover and watch, but when he shooed her away she started going through the letters.

There was nothing from Carlotta's day, but they were old. There was a bundle of letters from the turn of the century that her great-grandfather must have written to his young wife. She had flipped through, looking for dates and names, and then started to read one of these that started, 'My own beloved Anna,' and hesitated when she reached the end of the first page. The writing seemed laboured and the sentiments were stilted, but this was a true love letter, and she folded it again and put it down on top of the pile that had been fastened with a faded blue ribbon.

'Why the sigh?' David asked.

'Did I? They're all long after Carlotta.' She took out all that remained in the trunk, a large bound volume of the *Illustrated London News* for 1880, and began to replace the letters. 'They're love letters,' she said. 'What else do women keep?'

'You're not reading them?'

'Silly, isn't it?' She shut the lid and slipped down the clasp. 'But they'd depress me because I know the endings. I started on one that my grandfather's father wrote to his mother, and his father was lost at sea while my grandfather was a boy, so their love story didn't last. Nothing lasts, does it?'

'How do we know?' He looked at her steadily and her heart began beating in her throat. 'Since I met you,' he said, 'I'm changing my mind about all manner of things.'

'Oh?' But she didn't want him to tell her any more and she went on, 'I'll keep the books out and the old newspapers, and this scrapbook, of course, but I'll leave the letters in the trunk and I think I'll leave the trunk where it was.'

'You mean you want it back in the attic?' It was a battered old trunk, the attic was the place for it, and maybe some day she would read the letters.

'Yes, please,' she said.

The trunk was easier to handle with all the heavy books removed, but it was still cumbersome. They got it up the ladder, David taking the weight, and Felicity, carrying a torch, giving token assistance. 'Where it was, please,' she said when they were through the trapdoor, and she put down the torch and helped him carry the trunk to where it had made its impression in the dust and lower it, more or less, into the same spot.

In the lowering she must have overreached, or twisted, or done *something*, because a sudden sharp pain knifed through her, sending her sprawling over the trunk, gasping, 'Oh, my back, oh...!' It was excruciating. Tears sprang into her eyes and she couldn't believe it. She had never done anything like this before, she was agile and supple, but every time she moved the knife turned, and David had hold of her and he was asking,

'You're not fooling?' as though she might have been, although it would have been a silly sort of joke.

'*No!*' She gave a great dry sob. 'Of course I'm not, why should I be?' Then she remembered how they had smiled about Gordon's dodgy back, but this was no fooling, just coincidence and absolute agony. Serves me right, she thought, and groaned, 'How am I going to get down the ladder?'

'Can you move?' She moved warily, giving little yelps when the pain came, but finally standing upright.

'It's better like this,' she realised. 'If I keep my back straight.'

'Come on, then, let's get you down.'

'What have I done?' How would he know? She didn't know herself, because she had surely done nothing that should have caused this. She walked stiffly to the trapdoor and went slowly down the ladder, while David supported her rung by rung, and shouted for Mrs Clemo when he had Felicity leaning still and straight, like a dummy, against the wall.

Mrs Clemo hurried out of one of the rooms and Felicity told her, through clenched teeth, 'I've ricked my back. I can hardly move.'

'That was a stupid thing to do,' Mrs Clemo scolded,

as if Felicity had done it on purpose, and Felicity
wailed,

'I didn't do anything! We were putting the trunk back
and I leaned over and this happened.'

'Shouldn't have fetched it down in the first place,'
said Mrs Clemo. 'We'll never get the doctor out here
this morning.'

'Why not?' David helped Felicity take faltering steps
into her room and advised her, 'Better lie down on the
floor until we can find something hard and flat for the
divan. You can't have slipped a disc or you wouldn't be
able to stand upright, but you've probably given
yourself a bad sprain. Why can't we get the doctor out?'

'Because he won't see seventy again,' said Mrs
Clemo. 'He'd never get over the rocks.'

'Then I'll find someone who can,' said David. 'Do
you have any painkillers?' Mrs Clemo went to a drawer
and produced a packet of aspirins, and brought back a
pillow which she eased gently under Felicity's head. By
now Felicity was stretched out full length on a rug with
Sam snuffling in her ear. While she lay like this all she
felt was a dull and bearable ache, but she daren't sit up
and she hesitated about raising her head for the aspirins
and a gulp of water.

The aspirins went down, after a brief coughing fit,
and Mrs Clemo, over her first shock and collecting her
wits, told David, 'Old Dr Logan's the only doctor in the
cove, but there's others in the phone book. Or you
could try for Nurse Willcock, Anchor Cottage, next to
the post office up the hill.'

'Could somebody call Sam off?' Felicity begged
plaintively.

Sam thought this was a game. As fast as he was
pushed away he tried to dodge back, until Mrs Clemo
grabbed his collar and hauled him out of the room.

'How does it feel now?' David bent over Felicity and she could see the darker flecks in his grey eyes. He looked so concerned that she smiled to reassure him.

'I'm sure I'm not a stretcher case. I've only pulled a muscle, but I would like somebody to tell me exactly what I have done and what I'd better be doing about it. I can't lie here for long, can I?'

He brushed her hair back with a light reassuring touch. 'Don't run away,' he said, and his voice dropped for her alone, 'because I think I love you.'

'I think I'm pleased about that,' Felicity whispered back. When you were helpless it was a comfort to have someone tell you they thought a lot about you. It meant you could try to relax and leave them to deal with your problems.

David set off to get medical help and Mrs Clemo started to hunt around the house for something that could make a flat hard bed, and Felicity began flexing her muscles, trying to discover just how much damage she had done. She worked out which movement pierced her; she could put her hand on the spot and if she kept it pressed there the pain lessened.

It was nasty but not crippling, and she was tottering across to the divan when Mrs Clemo came back into the room and demanded, 'And where do you think you're going?'

'Not far,' Felicity reassured her, easing herself on to the divan, 'but I'm not keen on lying on the floor with my eyes closed, even if Sam has gone with David. I keep expecting spiders to sidle up to me.'

She pushed a cushion under the small of her back and asked, 'Did you find anything?'

'There are a few boards on the rocks,' said Mrs Clemo, 'that used to be the landing stage,' and Felicity sighed and wondered how long this pulled muscle would plague her. It meant no running up and down stairs or carrying heavy weights. No sudden movements or vigorous exercises, like painting ceilings—or *making love*!

She blinked as that thought occurred, because if she was looking for an excuse to avoid letting David make love to her, she had one now. This was a nuisance and it hurt, but it would give her time to decide whether she should risk a full passionate sexual relationship. If he put his mind to it he might be very hard to resist, she might have been swept off her feet; but now she could hold back and know that he wouldn't pressure her.

Every cloud has a silver lining, she thought, I'm almost lucky this happened. A few more days and I ought to know my own mind.

David brought Nurse Willcock back with him. Middle-aged, pink-cheeked and cheerful, she had enjoyed being helped over the broken causeway by a strong and handsome man. She examined Felicity and pronounced no bones out of place, but a badly pulled muscle when she prodded and Felicity yelled. She was not at all surprised it had happened so easily. You could pull a muscle any time. She had had patients who had been sitting in armchairs and got up and found they were in agony, and the treatment was rest, sleep on a board—or failing that the floor—and take painkillers if it got too bad or you couldn't take it easy. But it was nothing to worry about. So long as you were sensible it would heal itself.

'I'll see she takes it easy,' said David.

'I can see I'm leaving you in good hands,' Nurse Willcock twinkled, and accepted David's offer to see her back safely to the harbour wall.

While she lay waiting for his return this time Felicity's spirits began to sink. Until now the adrenalin of shock had been coursing through her, but all of a sudden depression set in. She was naturally energetic, enforced rest would come hard, and there was so much she wanted to do right now. She wanted to get things moving, and how could she when she could hardly move herself? Disappointment and frustration settled on her like a black cloud, and when she closed her eyes a tear squeezed between her lashes.

Jessie came back with David, and ran upstairs ahead of him into the Captain's Room, asking, 'And what have you been doing to yourself?' smiling because it wasn't that terrible. But when she saw Felicity's wet cheeks Jessie stopped smiling and began to console her, 'Don't upset yourself, you'll soon be all right. Nurse Willcock says it's only a strain.'

'I know,' Felicity sniffed, and rubbed the tears away quickly before David could see how upset she was. 'But there's so much I want to do, and at the best I'm going to be hobbling around for days.'

'What do you want to do that Mother and I can't do for you?' Jessie asked, and grinned as David took Felicity's hand. 'Well, most things.'

It was good to hold David's hand. Felicity wouldn't have minded him lying down beside her and putting his arms around her, and maybe she hadn't needed time to decide whether she wanted him or not. Maybe she did, and tonight they would have made love and it would have been glorious.

'Oh hell,' she said. 'Oh, I am sorry.'

'So am I.' He smiled at her. 'But we've got all the time in the world, and don't think I won't be waiting. In the meantime, what do you want doing for Gull Rock House?'

That made Felicity laugh and declare, 'I feel like

Scarlett when Rhett Butler told her to go ahead and fix up Tara!'

Within hours it seemed that half Trevarrow's Yard had commissions. The bedrooms were getting their patch-work quilts, rooms were to be decorated—she had opened on a budget too tight for anything but essentials and some of the decor was dingy. Somebody was framing the contents of the scrapbook, somebody else was painting the sea-witch on the van. In the next few days the house seemed full of callers, all of them delighted that Felicity had found a man to invest in her guest-house and that their own skills were in demand.

Felicity was in her element. Her helpers were her friends, and nobody was out to rook her. Besides which, David was nobody's fool, he got the terms right, and it was all down in black and white and she would pay him back, of course.

He painted the picture of the sea-witch himself. It was the girl in the old photograph, but it was also Felicity, her colouring, her sea-green eyes, although Carlotta had probably had dark hair and olive skin. She was holding a shell, which was a nice touch. When David suggested it Felicity said, 'Of course. I always used to take a shell back to school with me and listen to the sea in it. It was my good luck, my talisman. Of course she must be holding a shell.'

Arthur and Margie called to bring the miniature of William Mayne, and the oil painting of the Captain, and there were congratulations all round because they had produced two fine portraits. They were surprised at the sea-witch. Margie gasped, 'But it's *good*! You really can paint, can't you?' and Arthur wasn't flattering when he offered to handle any art work that David wanted to sell through his shop. Margie also said she was sorry to hear that Felicity had a bad back, she must have been up to something strenuous.

Everybody thought the strained muscle was a joke, and maybe it was, but it was inconvenient and it was taking its time getting better. At the end of a week Felicity was still moving carefully, sleeping on two boards, and David had been very understanding. It had been a passionately platonic period, with a lot of loverlike talk, mostly lighthearted, but no more. Although she was sure as could be that the moment she took any kind of initiative his response would be overwhelming.

She didn't see Gordon again, but she heard from the others that he was resentful about developments here. He considered himself hard done by, and the Galleries would be taking no more of Felicity's sea-spells. Felicity couldn't blame him. His pride was hurt and she was sorry, but she wasn't capable yet of driving into Fenmouth to see him and explain; and when she did she doubted if she could appease him, so she tried to put Gordon out of her mind. As life was a whirl of exciting activity these days it wasn't too difficult.

David had contacted some of his friends and colleagues. Several T.V. celebrities had agreed to come and sample Gull Rock House cuisine as soon as it reopened for business, and several journalists had promised publicity. The local paper, the *Penrann Telegraph*, had already run a story, with a photograph of Felicity and a potted 'history' of the house, featuring the legend of the sea-witch.

Except for her back Felicity had a fantastic two weeks, and she woke this morning feeling as good as new, with hardly a twinge left. They had placed the oil painting of her grandfather over the fireplace and each morning it seemed that he smiled at her and it was a blessing on her day. She felt that he looked particularly cheerful this morning. The sea-witch was finished too, but still on the easel because the lounge, where it was to hang, had stripped walls, and was half way through being re-painted.

Felicity worked at her desk till lunchtime dealing with the mail, and in the afternoon went for a walk alone along the beach, gathering scraps for her sea-spells. She had used up the last collection she had acquired on the day of the storm, when David had accompanied her. Today he was doing some work of his own, in his bedroom, and after lunch she took her basket and went beachcombing with Sam, enjoying feeling well and strong again.

She made it a leisurely stroll, and at one stage sat down on the shingle and threw sticks for Sam, looking back at the causeway, which had been repaired, and thinking how lucky she was and thanking the stars that had brought David to her door. Tonight she would tell him that she had carried the basket of pebbles with no trouble at all and what did he think about that? She could get rid of the boards on her bed now and maybe they could carry on from where he had looked at her and said, 'I think I love you.'

The two brothers who were decorating the lounge were packing up for the day when she wandered back into the house. 'Somebody to see you,' they told her together, and Alan, who had an eye for the girls, leered, 'A real cracker, name of Deirdre.'

'You'd better get up there fast,' said his brother, grinning. 'She's been with David for the past hour.'

CHAPTER SEVEN

COLD cut through Felicity. Alan and Anthony went on talking, the buzz of their voices followed her as she walked towards the staircase. She didn't want to climb those stairs and when she got up there she would probably lock herself in the first room and sit and wonder what she was going to say.

She should have told David ages ago how well she knew Deirdre. She could have done, and explained why she hadn't admitted it at first, and it would have been all right. He might have been briefly annoyed, but it would have been no big thing. Not then it wouldn't, but now that Deirdre was here and they'd had over an hour for talking things over, how could she explain? And hiding in bedrooms was no answer.

She opened the door and let Sam charge ahead of her and race over to David, who for the first time took no notice of him. Deirdre was lounging in an armchair looking sensational, with her pale perfect face and the black wings of her hair falling from the centre parting. She was wearing a short dark mink jacket over a beautifully cut grey suit, and boots, the exact shade of her coat, in soft shining leather.

One look at Deirdre made Felicity feel like something washed up by the tide. 'Hello,' she heard herself say idiotically. 'This is a surprise.'

'How could you?' Deirdre's voice throbbed, and Felicity realised she was still clutching her basket. She put it on a chair and began, 'I suppose I should have written to you.' She looked at David. 'And I should have explained to you.' He was sitting opposite Deirdre, with an expression that told Felicity nothing.

'But——' Felicity began.

'You pretended you didn't even *know* me!' Deirdre couldn't have looked more wounded if someone had tried to murder her. 'You let me talk about David and then when he turned up here you used everything I'd told you to get him interested in you.'

She couldn't deny it. She said, 'I suppose so. At first,' and David drawled,

'So much for instant rapport. I must be going soft in the head!'

'They say all's fair in love, but this wasn't love, was it?' Deirdre shuddered as though the sight of Felicity turned her stomach. 'This was such a cheap, mean little scheme! Just to turn your miserable little boarding-house into a money-maker. You worked for that from the moment David turned up here, didn't you?'

'*No!*' Felicity was stung into putting her side. 'What I started to do—it was a cheek, it was none of my business, but I thought you'd had a bad deal and I'd settle the score if I could.' Again she looked at David and again he looked back with hooded eyes. 'I started with the idea of leading you on, then letting you down. You hurt Deirdre and—well, I suppose at first I wanted to hurt you.'

He seemed to consider that, then he said, 'And the moral indignation vanished in a flash when I showed an interest in this place?'

It hadn't. She had still believed he was a womaniser, not to be trusted, but she had thought she could listen to a little business advice. Then somehow things had changed. She stammered, 'I thought——' but he ignored her, asking Deirdre,

'Did I treat you badly?' and incredibly Deirdre said

with sweet sadness, 'I thought you loved me and you didn't. That was the only way you hurt me. I was a bit down when I came here——'

'A *bit down*?' Remembering how Deirdre had carried on, the trouble she had had with her, Felicity blurted, 'You were suicidal!'

'I was not!'

'With some reason, as you thought you were pregnant.'

'*What*?' Deirdre squeaked.

'And you threw yourself off the landing stage and I had to pull you out.'

Deirdre was choking on her protests, 'You're making it up, all of it—I've always hated water, I'd never——'

Maybe it was an accident. Deirdre had drunk the best part of a bottle of wine that night. It had been late, she was tired, but she had gone into the water and Felicity had saved her from drowning. Now she was telling David, 'I've told you how it was. I came down here because I hoped you'd come, and I did talk a lot about you to Felicity, I thought she was my friend, so she knew all about you before she saw you. She knew who you were and that you'd got money, and she's broke and desperate about this house. She tried to get me to put some money in and become a partner because she's determined she's hanging on to it.'

True and false were getting so mixed up that there seemed no way to part them. Felicity had never suggested that Deirdre might invest in Gull Rock House, she had never let her pay a penny piece while she was here, but she had used what Deirdre told her about David.

'I asked you to send on any letters, I said if David ever called would you let me know. I can never forgive you for this!' Deirdre was lying now, and it was no use reminding her that she had left insisting she never wanted to hear his name again. She had obviously changed her mind on that, and looking seductive and sounding loving would be more likely to get him back than admitting she had nearly had a spectacular nervous breakdown after their last parting. It also made Felicity look a liar and a cheat.

Speechless, Felicity stared back at her and Deirdre nodded towards the painting on the easel. 'I like your picture,' she said. 'It's you all right—I told you David painted, didn't I? And about the Turner. All that. I like the shell too. We all used to think we heard the sea in a shell at school because you told us we could. You could always make people believe what you wanted them to.'

'You've made your point,' said Felicity. She wasn't proud of herself, she had been an idiot, but her dumbstruck stage was over. 'And it's still a fact that when you left here you said you never wanted to hear David's name again. You said it was finished, so you've got no call to blame me. And you——' She faced David and he shrugged in what appeared to be amiable disclaimer, declaring, 'I don't blame you. I think you're a conniving little bitch, but I admire singlemindedness, and you certainly know how to go about getting what you want.'

She felt as though he had struck her across the mouth, but she didn't flinch. 'I'll pay you back,' she said.

'You will.' He turned to Deirdre. 'Are you ready?' and she stood up as Felicity asked, 'Where are you going?'

'To find a hotel,' said David.

'I left too soon, didn't I? But now I'm here again I'm staying!' Deirdre put her hand through his arm and Felicity said, 'Goodbye then,' and went across to the desk, her back towards them, until David said, 'Don't run away.'

The last time he had said that he had added, 'Because I think I love you,' but this time his voice had a steeliness that made her shiver. 'Because we have some settling up to do.'

The door closed and Felicity went round the desk and sat down. That had been horrific, leaving her so depressed that she let her head fall on her folded arms, her hair spilling over them on to the desk. This house had always been the place she loved best, but now she longed to walk away from it. What was the use of struggling? What did anything matter anyway?

She raised her head and looked at the Captain's portrait over the fireplace, and thought it was lucky that Arthur and Margie had been paid. Lucky for them, but not so lucky for most of the others. The bill for the causeway had been met, but the new landing stage was not yet completed. Everything had been ordered in her name, all those commissions. David had promised her a loan for as much as she needed, but not in writing, and if he declined to pay up how was she going to manage?

She opened the drawer that contained the invoices and the lists. She had seen them all before, but now she went through them again, one by one. They didn't represent a fortune, but they might as well have done, because this was money she didn't have.

Jessie had warned her not to be greedy. The causeway was a necessity, and in the summer so was the landing stage, but there was no excuse for the extras, except that they would make Gull Rock House more attractive to the tourists. David had told her to go ahead and it had been lovely to take him at his word. Only now it was possible that he wouldn't pick up the tab.

He had said he admired her singlemindedness, but he

had called her a conniving little bitch and he wouldn't have been human if he hadn't resented being conned. So what could she do if he wouldn't lend her the money?

She was pretty sure the bank wouldn't advance this kind of overdraft without previous consultation. It sounded a rotten risk. She hadn't shown much business acumen, running up all these bills on somebody else's word of mouth. She had believed in David's word, but David had trusted her until the last hour or so, when he had run out of trust.

Felicity could think of no one else she could turn to. Money was tight everywhere. Gordon's family owned the biggest art shop in Fenmouth, but their profits were down too, and even when he was in love with her Gordon would never have helped to keep the guest-house going.

Last week she had moved his photograph from her desk into a cupboard, and now she took it out again and sat looking at it, trying to imagine herself asking this man if he would lend her enough to pay her creditors. But she couldn't for a moment see him doing that, and she put her photograph back in the cupboard.

So everything came full circle to David. When she saw him again she would apologise again if more apologies were wanted. After all, he had offered, she hadn't asked for a thing, and he hadn't walked out as though the deal was off. He had said he would be coming back, but not whether it would be tonight or tomorrow, and she had the impression that when he and Deirdre found that hotel they would both be booking in.

Her mind closed down on that like a shutter, because she had grown quite fond of David and the idea of him being with Deirdre hurt so that she couldn't bear to dwell on it.

She worked on her sea-spells for a while. She would have to ask Gordon if he would please let her have her old display stand back in the shop, and when she admitted she was desperate and she would be really grateful he probably would. But she wasn't getting her usual pleasure out of these little creations. They were no longer fun, they weren't even pretty, just cheap and tacky like Deirdre had described her, and David had agreed.

There was nothing cheap and tacky about Deirdre, which came of having wealthy parents. They had been short on love but lavish with material things, and Felicity had always thought that was sad. She had been sorry for Deirdre, but tonight Deirdre would have David, and whether he knew it or not he was heading for trouble there. And so was Deirdre, and goodbye and good luck to them both.

Felicity kept busy, almost in a state of controlled panic, going from room to room, doing unnecessary chores, dusting where there was no real need, polishing bits of silver and brass, killing time trying to tire herself so that she would sleep. By tomorrow's daylight her problems wouldn't seem so black, but tonight was hellish.

She heated a bowl of soup for her evening meal. She hadn't eaten since lunch, but after a couple of spoonsful her stomach heaved. Nerves probably, and she wouldn't wonder what David and Deirdre were eating. She wouldn't think about them, nor watch the clock as though she was expecting him back. She didn't want him back tonight. Tomorrow would be soon enough for that business talk and by tomorrow he might have calmed down.

It took her a long time to fall asleep, and she had no

idea how long she had been sleeping when Sam began barking. She sat up in bed, then got out, switching on the room light and tying the belt of her dressing gown as she went towards the door.

The moment she opened the door Sam shot out, and it might have been more sensible to have locked her door and stayed quiet, but it was too late for that now, so she crept along the corridor after him. If this was a break-in there wasn't that much worth stealing, and they wouldn't get her because she would be through a window into the sea. The water would be freezing cold, but she'd make it.

A light was on down there and Sam's barks were exuberant, and she called, 'David?'

'Who were you expecting?' He had a key and she hadn't fastened the bolts.

'Not you,' she said. 'I thought you'd be staying in the hotel.' That would be where Deirdre was and where he had stayed until now, whatever time now was.

'Sorry to disappoint you.' He began to climb the stairs while she stood at the top, trying to sound cool, asking,

'Why should I mind? Shall we talk?'

'By all means.' She led the way back into her room and he followed. As soon as she turned to face him he demanded, 'Why didn't you tell me you knew Deirdre?'

Felicity couldn't say, 'I was going to,' because she had had plenty of chances. She said, 'I don't suppose you'll believe this, but I think I forgot her,' and that was the truth, just as she had blocked Gordon out of her mind, but David said with sudden savage bitterness,

'Don't fence with me, or I shall get very rough.'

She had no doubt of that. She could sense his anger, and the effort with which he controlled it. She was no coward, but she was afraid, and she said desperately, 'I didn't ask you for anything. Not advice nor anything. You asked to see the books, you did the offering.'

He agreed grimly, 'I certainly did,' and she had to go on.

'So what happens now, because I've got bills I can't pay if you go back on our arrangement?'

He was so big and she felt small, tiny, so vulnerable that it was hard to stand straight and still and not cower. 'Nothing's changed,' he said. 'You keep your part of the bargain and I'll keep mine.'

That should have reassured her, but the knot of tension in her stomach tightened even more and she had to lick her lips before she could speak. 'We never got down to actual terms.'

'Oh yes, we did, clearly understood by both of us.' He eyed her from head to foot, and her bare toes clenched. 'You got the money and the publicity, I got you.'

'You're drunk,' she said, and he smiled, steady as a rock,

'I have never been drunk in my life.'

He was stone cold sober and she knew it, and there had been a time when she had wanted him to make love to her, but with tenderness, because he cared, not exacting payment. That was a monstrous suggestion. 'Well, I've been thick!' He went on, smiling, 'I actually believed you'd sprained your back!'

'I did.'

'I warned you, we're not playing games any more. You got the idea from your old boy-friend with the slipped disc. It was a better turn-off than a chastity belt.'

'You're unspeakable!' Felicity spat at him.

'But honest. You've cheated all along the line.'

'I hurt my back,' she said breathlessly. 'I don't know how, it was a surprise to me, I still can't understand how it happened, and I know we'd just been talking about Gordon, but that was a coincidence, and life's full of coincidences. It's a funny business, is life.'

'Shut up,' David said brusquely, and she closed her eyes when he came towards her. There was no chance of fighting him off physically, and she was fairly sure that he wouldn't rape her, although she believed he could carry this to the limits of humiliation. She didn't know where he would stop, she didn't know if he *would* stop.

I've called up the storm, she thought wildly, as he cupped her face in both his hands, his fingers pressing her skull so hard that her eyes opened in alarm and protest. 'You're a schemer,' he told her, 'but I won't allow you to be a welsher.'

'And what do you think you're going to do about it?' She shouldn't have said that. It sounded like a taunt, challenging the violence in him, when she should be pleading.

But she couldn't plead, whatever he did to her. His hands slid under her robe, tearing a thin strap of her nightdress as his mouth covered her parted lips with brutal suddenness. The hard pressure of his body was sensitising every part of her. There was no tenderness, no liking, but a searing, soaring passion that terrified her because this fevered desire was her own reaction.

She had to deny it, to herself and to him, keeping rigid against him until every muscle ached. Fighting herself—don't give in, don't let it happen, don't let him know that you would glory in it. An angry man, despising you, how can you want him so badly that if he takes you by force it will only be moments before you are giving willingly, and taking, matching his savagery, out of your mind?

When he almost loosed her she moaned, biting her lower lip, and he held her at arm's length, surveying her with a cool weighing look. 'For a girl who makes capital out of her sexuality,' he told her, 'you've got a problem. But you can relax tonight. I prefer some sophistication in my partners. Breaking and entering is not my style.' He let her go. 'Goodnight,' he said, and went without a backwards glance.

Even when she was quite alone Felicity stayed taut, as though she was holding back pain. She took off her robe and dropped it where she stood, then hitched her nightdress on the side the shoulder strap had broken. She looked at the clock and it was coming up to four, so he had as good as spent the night with Deirdre. No wonder this had been a threat rather than the real thing! He probably needed his sleep rather more than he needed Felicity. Deirdre would have been both sophisticated and eager, and a sound like a sob burst from Felicity.

She picked up the nearest thing, the little travelling clock in a leather case, and hurled it at the easel and the painting whose enigmatic shadow of a smile was maddening her. It was of herself, smug and silent when she should at least have been telling David about Deirdre, because any fool could have known that he would find out. If Felicity could have called back time she would have started off telling him, and maybe he wouldn't have stayed longer than that first night, nor offered any help with Gull House. Or maybe he would, because right from the first there had been electric awareness between them.

But she couldn't call time back. All she had done for time was smash the clock, which had stopped ticking, although the smiling sea-witch was unmarked. Even by daylight there was no sign of as much as a dent. Felicity was examining the canvas when David knocked on her door, wearing a blue mohair sweater and navy slacks, cool as a cucumber, looking as though he had slept well and dreamlessly.

Felicity had hardly slept at all, but now she was dressed neatly, in jeans and a thick-knit cream Arran sweater, hair brushed and face made up. She had put on her make-up in here because after last night she didn't fancy facing him barefaced. She could either blush scarlet or go sickly pale, she needed a mask of cool colour.

'Good morning,' he said. 'Anything wrong with it?'

She had taken the picture to the window and been relieved that it was undamaged, it would have been hard explaining why she had hurled the clock. David didn't sound angry this morning. Yesterday might never have happened, but it had, and yesterday had to change everything.

She said, for something to say, 'It should be dark hair, she was Spanish.'

'Then darken it yourself,' he said, and as she said, 'Sorry, I shouldn't be quibbling,' he grinned, nicely this time, ruefully but with no bitterness.

'I'm not a good loser,' he said. 'You outmanoeuvred me, and why not? That's what life's all about.'

He didn't sound resentful, just realistic, but she had to protest, 'I really didn't set out to get you to back this place, I just thought you'd handed Deirdre a bad deal——'

'Some might say you'd done the same for Gordon.' His amusement sounded genuine this morning, and although her affair with Gordon had never approached passionate commitment some folk might think she had treated him badly. Gordon did himself, and perhaps it was hypocritical, her blaming David for cooling off Deirdre when she had cut Gordon out of her life completely for the last two weeks.

'Out of interest,' said David, 'did you ever want to buy a Turner?'

'Now what would I do with a Turner?'

'I should have suspected.' He took the sea-witch from her and put it back on the easel and shook his head—not at the painting but at his own obtuseness. 'It was too pat. Our tastes tallied too well.' He grinned, 'You even read Tolstoy. Now that can't be true.'

'I saw the film *War and Peace*,' she said, 'but for a read I'll take Ed McBain or a good romance any day.' She could still make him smile, but it was different this morning. He was no longer sore about her cheating him, and of course she had in a way, but she knew that he hadn't come in here to make trouble.

Nor to try to make her; she knew that too. She could still see him as a dangerously desirable man, but he represented no danger to her because, quite simply, he did not want her.

She began, 'About last night——' and his mouth quirked, admitting a con trick at his expense, 'I think we'd better forget our original "understanding",' and she *had* led him on, at first with calculated charm and he thought it was calculated all along. It wasn't, but he was never going to believe that, and she should be grateful he didn't seem to mind too much. 'It seems,' he said, 'you're either a very determined virgin or frigid as far as I'm concerned, and I'm too old and too cold to deal with either.'

He was thirty-four and the truth was that he didn't feel that getting Felicity to bed would be worth the trouble. He had Deirdre now, of course, and Felicity's mouth was so dry that it tasted of dust and ashes. She croaked, 'Are you going away, then?'

'No, I'll keep my room, if that's all right. I've started getting down to work, my kind of work. If you agree

I'll get a lawyer friend to look over the books, and the bills, and we'll work out how much you can pay back on a monthly basis when the profits start coming in.'

'That sounds perfect.' It was what she would have done anyway, but it would have been a lot more perfect if Deirdre had stayed in France. 'You won't be disturbed here,' she said. 'There'll be nothing to distract you.'

'No.'

'About Deirdre.' She shouldn't but she plunged on, 'If you're starting that up again think twice before you finish it again, because when she came down here she *was* suicidal.' He gave her a flat hard stare that made her stammer, 'Sorry, it isn't my business.'

'No, it is not.' As the door closed quietly behind him Felicity gave a long shuddering sigh because it was as though the door had slammed in her face, shutting her off from everything that made life worth while.

She had to get moving, get earning. Get the lounge finished and the customers in. The Taylor brothers' van was parked on the sea-front, she met them on the causeway and hailed them breezily, 'Can you hurry it up, I want to open as soon as possible?'

They had worked fast, it had been a big job—most of the house; the lounge was last on the list. But the sooner they were through the sooner they would get paid and they could use the money. They would work overtime tonight if that was what Felicity wanted. 'I've been doing next to nothing for nearly two weeks,' she explained, 'and now my back's clicked back, or whatever, I want to get cracking.'

'Is Deirdre still there?' Alan enquired. They had both been impressed and wondered if she was an actress or a model, asking after David Holle and hurrying upstairs smiling when they told her where to find him.

'No,' said Felicity. 'She just dropped in. I used to go to school with her.'

'She said her name was Deirdre Osborne,' said Anthony, 'but she didn't ask for you.'

'Well, schooldays were a long time ago.'

The Taylors lived in Fenmouth, so it was possible that the news of David's caller had not yet gone round Tregorran Cove. Although her car might have been spotted, and so might she, coming alone, leaving with David. Felicity went up the hill to Jessie's house and caught Jessie clearing the breakfast table. 'All on your own?' she asked.

Jessie looked blank. 'Yes.' The children had gone to school and Jan was out with the fishing fleet. 'Why?'

'Deirdre turned up yesterday afternoon. Did you know?' There was no need to ask, Jessie's startled expression showed that this was a small bombshell to her. She had picked up the teapot to check if there was any tea left and she almost dropped it, gasping, 'Whatever brought her back?'

'Anything could have done. Anyone who knows David could have told her he was here and there was that article in the local paper and maybe other mentions. 'But——' Felicity winced, 'it didn't go down too well because I never did tell him I knew her. She did, though, of course, and that she talked about him to me non-stop all the time she was here. She said she asked me to let her know if he tried to get in touch with her after she'd left. She didn't,' she added quickly seeing Jessie wondering about that, 'but he thinks now that I deliberately set out from the beginning to catch him so that he'd put money into the guest-house.'

When Felicity paused Jessie drew in a deep breath, and let it out again, as though she couldn't find any words. Then she said hesitantly, 'Well, I suppose you did, really, didn't you?'

'Yes, but——' There was a 'but', her reasons hadn't been entirely mercenary, but all she could say now was, 'I needed that help. There was the causeway, and——'

'We didn't need the patchwork quilts and the dishwasher,' said Jessie. 'Nor all that decorating done.'

'You're right—I shouldn't have run up the bills, and things have changed now, and it's going to be on a very businesslike footing, and I've got to be showing a profit to make the repayments, so will you come back with me now and help me put things straight so we can open again?'

'All right,' said Jessie. 'How's your back?' She knew it had been getting better, this morning Felicity had forgotten it completely, there wasn't even a twinge. She wriggled now and smiled wryly.

'Better, and that was something else. David's convinced now that I faked it to stop him trying to make love to me.'

'Did you?' asked Jessie bluntly, and Felicity shook her head.

'It was just bad luck.' If it hadn't happened she knew that she and David could not have spent all those nights alone together in Gull House without becoming lovers. If they had she might have told him about Deirdre, or when Deirdre came it might not have mattered because surely the bond then would have been strong enough to withstand anything. But they were not lovers, never had been and never would be. He was Deirdre's lover and that hadn't counted for much with him, so perhaps Felicity was lucky to escape uncommitted.

'I said, "Where's Deirdre now?"' said Jessie, obviously repeating herself, and Felicity blinked, clearing her head of whirling thoughts,

'She went to a hotel. They both did, although David came back this morning and he's keeping on his room. He's working on his script or whatever it is now.'

Jessie took the teapot into the kitchen and emptied it. 'Won't be a sec,' she said. 'I'll just swill these.' She washed up quickly. 'I must say, though,' she said, 'it's going to look all right. It's going to be a super little place, and the paintings are lovely—the Captain and that one of you.'

'You mean Carlotta.'

'He's painted that lovely,' said Jess. She got into her coat and asked, making it sound casual, 'How did he take it?'

'Very well.' Felicity smiled and caught a glimpse of herself in the mirror over the fireplace of the living room and thought how false the smile looked. 'He's a very civilised man,' she said. 'He said I knew how to go about getting what I wanted and he admired singlemindedness.' Jessie stood in the kitchen door, watching her, and Felicity admitted, 'He was very angry. Not this morning. This morning he's civilised. He says I cheated, but he thinks he was a fool not to have seen through me, but it doesn't seem to be bothering him this morning. Last night, though—well, he came back about four o'clock, and I thought he was going to——' she gave a nervous little laugh—'get rough.'

'What do you mean, get rough?' asked Jessie.

'You know, beat me up.' She didn't say 'rape me', although that had been the threat and Jessie would have understood why it had. 'Take what had seemed to be on offer from the first night he came here', would have been the truth. She had never feared a blow, she had known he wasn't going to 'beat her up', but she didn't want to say anything that would bring back memories of his crushing arms around her and the wild tumult of her own emotions.

'But he didn't?' said Jessie.

'No. I suppose he decided it wasn't worth the trouble.'

'You were lucky.'

'I was,' Felicity agreed.

'And another thing,' said Jessie, 'I'm glad you were only thinking about the business. If you'd really fallen for him I'd be ever so sorry about this.' Jessie had seen Felicity was growing fond of David, and if he had taken up with Deirdre again she had hoped it wasn't going to hurt Felicity too much. But Felicity sounded bright enough, hastening to assure her, 'Now that's where I was really lucky, because he's stopped being narked this morning, but it's put him off me for good and ever.' She grimaced, then grinned, and Jessie smiled and hoped that this was no act.

Felicity's convalescence was over. It was fortunate that Deirdre hadn't turned up before. That might have stopped Felicity running up some of the bills, but her pulled muscle had had time to mend and she could spring into work and activity. She was opening again as soon as possible with bargain breaks, parties, bar trade, meals, anything. She had good menus planned and the house had never looked so inviting, nor been so exciting, with the legend of the sea-witch that David had written up for the leaflets that were printed and waiting.

The Taylor brothers were busy in the lounge, and that day Felicity and Jessie and Mrs Clemo put the other rooms in order, including the sea-witch's room, which had been decorated in pale greens and blues. Felicity had already chosen the room she would be using as bedroom-cum-office and she started moving out of the Captain's Room.

David opened his door on to the corridor as she staggered past with a huge load of clothes, and she explained, 'I'm moving rooms. They'll have the lounge finished by tonight, so I can get the bar and the dining room open.'

'What are your terms for the Captain's Room?'

'You know.' While she was immobilised she had worked out costs and charges, keeping prices as low as possible because anything else would have been stupid.

'I'll take it for a month,' he said.

'Just for you?' The words popped out. With the big desk in it would be ideal for his work—but it was the biggest upstairs room, and she had expected to let it mainly to couples. Of course it was just for him, he wouldn't be likely to be bringing Deirdre here. Somebody else maybe—that thought made her wince. 'Oh, damn!' she exclaimed, as half her load slithered out of her grasp. David picked up the clothes and replaced them in her arms.

'Glad to see the improvement in your back's being maintained,' he said gravely, and she muttered, 'Not as glad as I am,' and continued on her way because a recurrence of that was all she needed.

He hadn't answered her question whether he intended sleeping alone in the Captain's Room, and she wouldn't think about it. She'd know soon enough and it was none of her business.

Downstairs they all ate lunch in the kitchen: Mrs Clemo and Jessie, the Taylor brothers and Felicity; a pile of ham sandwiches and slices of pork pie, washed down with tea or beer, and got back to work as soon as possible. But Felicity took a tray up to David.

Mrs Clemo hadn't mentioned Deirdre, although Jessie had taken her on one side and Felicity suspected she was still making up her mind whether to say, 'What did I tell you?' or sympathise. If Felicity had shown any signs of distress Mrs Clemo would have grieved for her, but as she didn't Mrs Clemo settled for, 'I don't know. One of these days, my girl.'

I shall call up the storm, thought Felicity. I did, but it's blown over now. I think it's blown over.

'Do you want me to take this up?' Jessie suggested when David's luncheon tray was laid, but Felicity picked it up,

'That's all right, I want a word with him.' None of them guessed how her heart was thumping and that she would rather have let Jessie take the tray and kept out of his way, but if he was staying on she must steel herself to meeting him and talking with him. She had to carry on as though he was just another customer who happened to be a business colleague, but she needed a moment to stiffen her courage outside his door before she balanced the tray and knocked.

'Food,' she said, carrying it in.

'Thanks.' He was sitting at the little writing table, with a rather battered old typewriter, a pocket tape-recorder and a pile of papers. Felicity set down the tray on a chair and asked, 'How's it coming?'

'Not badly.' If he was stopping to eat she wasn't disturbing his creative mood, and she hovered.

'This is the TV script with the Cornish background, is it, that you came down to Padstow to write?'

'Yes, and sorry, but I can't give Gull Rock House a mention in it.' He was joking, but she blushed.

'What is it about?'

He leaned back, flexing his shoulders. They were broad, the muscles were smooth and there was a long scar on his left shoulder that he'd got falling into a glass frame in a garden as a boy. Deirdre had told her about that, she had never seen it herself. 'You're my number one fan,' he said. 'You've read all my books, you've seen all my TV programmes, you know the kind of scripts I write.'

'Well——' she began, and he grinned.

'Only you don't do you? I bet you've never read one of my books.'

'I've got friends who have. I *have* seen——'

'Looking out for my name in the credits.' He was mocking himself for having swallowed that. 'And here was I thinking what a critic you were going to be! Ask her to read it, I thought, ask her what she thinks of it so far.'

'What's it about?' She would have got his books out of the library days ago if she had had the chance. She had wanted to read them, and she would have liked to hear about this script now, but he said drily,

'Don't push your luck, I'm not falling for the fan trick twice,' and she knew that he wanted neither her opinion nor her interest.

She went back to her own work because David did want repayment for his investment and the Taylor brothers finished the entrance lounge before they went home, and when Felicity fell into bed that night it was her last night in the Captain's Room and she was so exhausted she could have been drugged.

Next morning she went to the window, breathing in the salt air. Tomorrow her window would be smaller and would face Tregorran Cove, not the open sea. She wondered if David, and the paying guests who came after him, would stand here. They would spin the globe and look through the telescope, of course. They would be toys to them as they had been to her when she was a child.

She wondered if he would show a girl the mechanics of trying to adjust the lens. Deirdre was near here, but

she doubted if Deirdre would care to come back to Gull
Rock House. David had other women friends, of
course, famous, some of them, beautiful and clever.
Felicity wondered if he would bring one of them, to
show her that with all her cheating and conniving she
could never compete with the kind of girl he could get.

He wouldn't. Not for that reason. Any girl he
brought would be here for her own sake, nothing to do
with Felicity, and she turned away from the window,
almost falling over Sam because, suddenly, her eyes
were stinging and misting. She wondered whether Sam
would move into the little room with her, or stay in the
Captain's Room. She suspected that so long as David
was here, here he might stay.

'Anyhow, lovie,' she said to the painting on the easel,
'I'll take you downstairs with me and you can get used
to your new surroundings.' Carlotta's place was above
the big fireplace so that she presided over the entrance
lounge. Arthur and Margie were bringing a heavy old
gilt frame that would set off the painting beautifully
and when Felicity went downstairs she carried the
canvas with her.

These walls had gone through some changes over the
years. When they were stripped Felicity had recognised
a wallpaper that her grandmother had chosen. There
were others beneath it, and they had discussed the
possibility of finding a near-copy of one of them. In the
end they had stayed with plain white walls for this
room. That was how it had been for the last ten years,
but now the wall surface was stripped down to the basic
plaster and surface irregularities, the cracks and lumps
in the plaster gave it the genuine look of the original
house.

There were bright pretty old-new wallpapers in the
bedrooms and everywhere the paintwork was gleaming

fresh, and although it was going to take some paying back, Felicity couldn't hold down her pleasure. Like Jessie had said, Gull Rock House had been turned into a super little place. She put the painting in the wooden armchair and looked around, with a smile that widened. It was *lovely*! How she had always wanted it to be, and from the top of the stairs David asked, 'Satisfied?'

She had been grinning like a Cheshire cat. She must look madly smug. She said, 'Well, it is splendid, isn't it?'

'I don't know about splendid. But attractive, yes.'

'You can move into the big room today. Any time this afternoon.'

'Right.' He came down the stairs and his lack of interest in her was like a cool wind. She would serve breakfast now. They might eat it together, but nothing she could do or say would touch him, although they might talk in friendly fashion all the way through the meal. She had accepted that and she would serve him his meal alone, but she had to tell him she had decided to throw a re-opening party a week on Saturday. She crossed fingers, touching the armchair. 'And please, Lord, no storms. I know it's shortish notice, but everything's ready now and it gives me time to get some advertisements in the local papers and get in touch with some of my customers. Do you think—I mean, would you ask——'

'I'll get you your names,' he said. 'I've got an interest in this business too.' Not in her any more, but it was the business that mattered. He looked towards the painting and asked, 'When did Carlotta get washed up in the cove?'

'You know when.' She had told him, he had mentioned it in the leaflet.

'We don't have an actual date, though, do we? Just

the winter of 1868. So why not Saturday night for her anniversary?'

'It could be.' That would make the legend seem more vivid and real. This very night ... 'What a brilliant idea,' she said enthusiastically, and put out a hand to touch his arm, and he moved away. It need not have been deliberate, but it made her feel rebuffed and ashamed.

He stood in front of the painting, viewing it with a slight frown, and she heard herself ask tartly, 'Planning changes?'

'The hair colour, you mean?'

'I wasn't actually thinking about that. Maybe it doesn't look sly enough, not sufficiently underhand and conniving. Maybe you should take it away and make it uglier.'

'Was she ugly?' he asked.

'That's a portrait of me there.' It was recognisable from the old daguerreotype, but also as Felicity, and it was a lovely face with a haunting magic. When David had painted that he had seen her through very different eyes from the cool gaze he turned on her now, and she said challengingly, 'If you'd like to put your fist through it go right ahead.' She hated being treated as though she was nothing, she would rather he had gone on being angry, and she almost ran at him and started beating clenched fists against him as though she was the injured one.

He laughed and shook his head at her. 'You're crazy,' he said. 'Can I have breakfast in about half an hour?' He went through the front door, and when he had gone Felicity realised that she was shaking. She had had a lucky escape last night, because then he had been angry enough to take her by force, and what did she think she was doing this morning? Goading him into violence? Her grandfather was right, there was a wild streak in her and unless she checked it she was heading for trouble, but it took her a good ten minutes to get herself together.

She must stop provoking David. She had a hundred things to do and she must keep her mind on them. Today she would plan a buffet for the Night of the Sea-Witch, phone and write around. She had already written to Edward Cunliffe to cancel his booking, 'Because I'm closing temporarily for improvements.' She would write again now and say how delighted she would be to see him because things had moved faster than she had expected and Gull Rock House would be back in business within days.

She would post off leaflets with a letter to 'old customers' who had gone away promising to come back next year. Maybe they would come sooner, if it was only for a meal or an overnight stay. And, if she had time, she would call on Gordon and ask him if he would please go on selling the sea-spells, and show him the leaflet and invite him to the re-opening.

When David returned she served up breakfast. She didn't eat with him and he didn't suggest that he might. He had brought the *Telegraph* and he read that, and when she took away the bacon-and-eggs plate and set down the toast she asked, 'Will you be here for lunch?'

'Yes, but anything will do. Just a tray in my room, I'll be working.'

'Dinner?'

'No.' He would be dining with Deirdre, of course, and she wouldn't say, 'How about tomorrow's breakfast?' because that would be provocative, so she said nothing. She went back into the kitchen and stayed there, until through the crack in the door she saw him leave the dining room.

There was a chance that Gordon wouldn't see her. She
had put the Galleries at the end of her list, and when
she walked into the shop in the late afternoon, she
could feel the eyes of every assistant on her. Gordon
was showing two customers some porcelain figures of
birds. A robin, a blue-backed house martin and a pied
warbler, had been placed on the glass top of the
counter, and a man and a woman were looking down at
them with frowning concentration.

Gordon saw Felicity appear at the counter and then
he frowned too, and she smiled, appeasingly she hoped,
and nodded towards his office door. After a few
seconds he nodded and she went into the office to wait
for him.

The Galleries had been one of her best outlets, she
didn't want to lose that. Nor did she want to lose
Gordon's friendship, there was no reason why they
should be on bad terms. 'Hello, stranger,' he said as he
came into the room, and this time it was not an
endearment.

'I've been housebound,' she explained. 'I pulled a
muscle getting that trunk back into the attic.'

'I heard about it.' He didn't sound particularly
sympathetic. 'And I heard about the money that's being
spent on your place. You managed things very nicely
there.'

'It does look nice,' Felicity agreed, as if he had meant
it as a compliment. She was seated, but Gordon stayed
on his feet, moving restlessly around, demanding,

'Has he moved in permanently?'

'David?' Of course, David. 'Just a few weeks. He
wanted somewhere quiet down here, where he could
work.'

'Are you sleeping with him?'

'No.'

'Are you going to?'

'I told you,' she said, 'it's a business arrangement. He has a girl-friend, several probably, and I have a business. I sleep well, and alone, at nights, so that I can be alert and businesslike all day long.' She got the glimmer of a smile from him for that. 'So please will you go on selling my sea-spells, because of course I've got to pay all this money back?'

After that Gordon was more amenable. He hadn't yet dismantled the display of her work in the Galleries, and he agreed to leave it where it was, and put a few leaflets about Gull Rock House and the sea-witch beside it. He even said he would come to the reopening and wished her luck. As the lesser of two evils he preferred her to be obsessed with the guest-house rather than with David Holle.

'Are you doing anything tonight?' he asked as she rose to leave, and she said quickly, 'I'm up to my eyes in work.'

'You would be, of course.' He had heard that excuse so often since she started taking in paying guests.

'But I will be in touch,' she promised. 'And thank you, and do come over.'

'Yes,' said Gordon. 'Yes.' He would, he supposed, because there was something about Felicity that would always fascinate him.

She went out to her van, with the sea-witch motif, in the car park, and sat for a while composing herself. When she came here she had thought that, if things went well, she might be spending the evening with Gordon. He had been her very good friend, and if he was willing she had thought he might be again. She liked Gordon very much and now she was on her way back home, to an empty house and work that could easily wait till tomorrow.

Why? she wondered; and knew it was because she didn't want to be with any man but David. David wouldn't be waiting for her, but that made no difference. He was still the only one, and when he was not there she would wait.

I love him, she realised in sudden and sickening despair—really love him, and he thinks I'm a cheat and a grabber, and he will never trust me again, much less love me, and there isn't any hope at all.

CHAPTER EIGHT

I LOVE him terribly, Felicity thought, and it shouldn't have surprised her. From the beginning there had been that strong current of awareness between them, and in these past few weeks David had coloured her life and her thoughts as though they had been inseparable for years. She couldn't imagine now being without him, and that was what Deirdre had said—'He made himself my life.'

Perhaps he always did that, with the woman of the moment, and jealousy exploded inside her, making her grip the wheel of the car until her knuckles gleamed. She hadn't admitted jealousy before, but now the pictures came in brilliant harsh colour and detail: David and Deirdre, David and the others before Deirdre, splintering in her brain so that she had to stop seeing them before they sent her crazy.

She loosed the wheel slowly and pressed her hands together, palm to palm, resting her chin on her fingertips. She knew now why she had borrowed more from him than she need have done. Because the bigger his investment in Gull Rock House the less likely he would be to go away without coming back, and although he thought she was a cheat and a grabber he wasn't going away just yet, and she wouldn't believe that he didn't still want her. If she accepted that she would be cold and lonely for the rest of her life.

Someone tapped on the window and she saw one of the women assistants from the Galleries mouthing, 'Are you all right?' It was closing time, she must have been sitting out here for ages, so she wound down the window and said, 'Yes.'

'Only you'd got your eyes closed and you look awfully white. Are you waiting for him?'

'For Gordon? No. I—I've got a bit of a headache, but it's clearing now. Thanks.' Felicity turned on the ignition, and drove out of the car park. Home now, she supposed, although if David was there he would be getting ready to leave and meet Deirdre for dinner. Where? Felicity wondered. If the hotel was in Fenmouth it would probably be the Harbour Inn, which was new and plush, or the Grand, which was old and plusher, and she had a sudden wild notion of going searching for them, but that would be crazy. She couldn't imagine what she was about, and that was the trouble, she wasn't thinking clearly.

She concentrated on her driving, in this state it would have been easy to misjudge speed and cause an accident; but she really didn't feel up to tackling the drive home just yet, so she parked in the road, near the entrance to Trevarrow's Yard. There were at least half a dozen shops and studios in there where someone would give her a cup of coffee and she could sit and chat and listen and wait until her nerves steadied before she faced the rest of her journey.

She wouldn't have to explain why she had called,

because this was a little conclave of friends. Some were very good friends, like Margie and Arthur, but she couldn't tell even Margie, 'I've just had a shock. I seem to have fallen in love without realising it was happening until it all went wrong, and I don't know what to do, because I think I've ruined everything.'

She made for their shop. The Closed sign was turned outwards on the door, but Margie was replacing a painting in the window that someone had asked to examine during the afternoon and hadn't bought. She smiled and waved at Felicity, and Felicity waved back. 'Come for the frame?' asked Margie, opening the door. 'We were bringing it over tomorrow.'

'Well, I was here,' said Felicity, 'so I thought I might as well.'

'On your own?'

'Yes.'

'You don't have to rush off?'

'No.'

'Good-oh,' said Margie, leading the way upstairs to their studio-living room where Arthur was cleaning a Victorian oil painting, and the sharp odour of varnish stripper mingled with woodsmoke. 'Hello,' said Arthur, looking up from his work and waiting to see if anyone else was following. 'All by yourself?'

'Yes,' said Felicity. She usually was, but now they had expected David to be with her, and she thought how sad the words sounded . . . On your own . . . all by yourself . . .

They never had before. At home she had missed her grandfather desperately, but around and about she had always felt complete and confident. Losing David would be like losing an arm—worse; eyes, maybe. Half of the oil painting was a dark and murky landscape, while the cleaned portion showed blue skies, and her lips twisted in a wry smile. That's the difference, she thought, and said, 'My goodness, it looks like two pictures.'

'Mmm, it is coming up rather well.' Arthur sounded pleased with himself. 'Where's David?'

'Taking somebody out to dinner,' said Felicity, sounding, she hoped, as though that was quite all right by her, but Margie asked sharply,

'Another girl?'

'Yes.' They had been at the engagement party the night Deirdre went into the sea, but they had never met her, nor heard about her, and it was too tangled a tale to start telling now.

'Business?' Margie hoped it was. She had been so sure that David and Felicity were made for each other, but Felicity smiled steadily.

'I'm business. The guest house is business. And by the way, I'm opening again a week on Saturday. You will come to my opening, won't you?'

Of course they would. 'We've decided,' she said, 'that this could be the very night Carlotta got washed up, so it all ties in nicely.'

They could see that. Margie loved a party, Arthur could take them or leave them, and Margie loved the idea of the sea-witch too. '*Could* she cast spells?' she asked now. 'Really?'

'They said so,' said Felicity. 'It's in the leaflets.' David had made a good story out of the old tales, the village under the sea, the sea-witch, and Arthur chuckled,

'Not his usual line, was it?'

'I suppose not.' Felicity hesitated. 'Would you—have any of his books?'

Arthur had told David he'd read and liked them, but she was surprised when he said, 'Yes.'

'Could I borrow one?'

'Which would you like?'

'I haven't read any.' Arthur's eyebrows shot up at that, then he went over to a bookshelf and Margie asked,

'Have you ever tried to cast spells? You do look like her. It could be in the blood.'

'No such luck,' said Felicity. She wished it was. She knew the wish she would start with. That David should be waiting when she got home, and ready to listen to her. She wouldn't wish for him to love her, that would need too strong a spell. But if he would soften a little she would work on it with all her heart and soul.

'How about this one?' Arthur was handing her a book and she went to the sofa by the stove to look at it. The photograph on the back was the studio portrait that Deirdre had left behind, so Felicity could have destroyed that, it would have been easy enough to get another. She had hidden it in a drawer, and now she knew that she had always wanted to keep it.

She could have sat here, just looking at the photograph, touching the slightly ruffled hair, tracing the line of the strong sensual mouth, but Margie and Arthur were watching, so she turned the book and frowned, 'The title seems familiar. Wasn't it made into a film?'

'Of course it was,' said Arthur, as though he despaired of her ignorance, and she thought, He must make a lot of money, and he'll never believe I didn't know that from the beginning.

This was a thriller, set in Sardinia, and she put it down beside her, photograph up, and wished with love and longing that he would be there when she got back, and thought wryly, That should prove if I've any witch blood in me!

She stayed for a cup of tea and a slice of walnut cake, and they chatted about mutual interests and acquaintances. It was cosy, and Felicity knew that she was blessed in her friends. She felt calmer after half an hour or so, and excused herself, 'You can imagine what a lot I've still got to do,' put the frame in the van, and set off for Tregorran Cove.

It was silly, but the nearer she came to home the stronger grew her conviction that it was going to be how she had wished. David would be there, and he would be prepared to listen to her. They said if you really believed something you could make it happen; think positively, they said and she did, all the way from Fenmouth.

But when she turned into the boatyard all the spaces under the sign Private Parking for Gull Rock House were empty, and disappointment deflated her like a pricked balloon. So much for the witch blood, she thought, and tried to laugh at herself, but she couldn't raise even the faintest smile.

David wasn't in the house. He wouldn't be, with his car gone, but as she opened the door and Sam came to greet her her home seemed as empty as in the early days after her grandfather's death, and she was fearful that this was how it would always be, wherever she went. That even in a crowded room, if David was not there, she would be alone.

She made a great fuss of Sam, petting him and talking to him. She stirred up the fire, and fixed the painting in its frame and hung it over the fireplace. It looked at home, she thought, and so it should be, as it was so nearly a picture of herself.

Then she went upstairs, and although she knew David wasn't here she tapped on the door of the Captain's Room. When there was no reply she walked in. He had moved in. His typewriter was on the desk, presumably his papers were in the drawers, and when she opened the cupboard where she had kept her clothes his hung there.

She touched the sleeve of a mohair jacket and found herself lifting it to her lips, then panicked that she might have left a lipstick smear. She hadn't, and she held it to her cheek for a moment, and the material felt like a light caress. If she closed her eyes she could pretend he was with her and he *was* coming back. He would be working and living in this room. He was involved in the re-opening of Gull Rock House, and somehow she must convince him that he had not been cheated.

She curled up in a chair, downstairs, in front of the fire, and started reading the book she had brought from Arthur's. From the first paragraph it was compulsive, completely absorbing, and it was only when Sam barked for his supper that Felicity realised it was bedtime and that she had stiffened up so that she felt a twinge from her pulled muscle.

She rubbed it and it went. Then she fed Sam, and afterwards strolled outside, watching the dog snuffling around the rocks. It was a still night. Moonlight flickered on the water, and window lights gleamed around the harbour and edged the winding ribbon of road up the hill.

Felicity took the book to bed with her, and read until her eyelids began to close. Then she shut the book and turned to the photograph on the back. She didn't kiss it, it was cold smooth paper and she yearned for a warm human touch, but she did whisper, 'Goodnight, my love,' when she switched out the light.

Sam, in unfamiliar surroundings, continued snuffling and pacing for a while, finally settling down in a disgruntled heap. Felicity was tired. She slept heavily at first but woke again within a few hours, and immediately her mind began racing, filling her with despair. Lying here, in the dark, there seemed no light and no hope. The man she ached for was out of her reach, tonight and every night, and frustration spread to every nerve until she was tossing like somebody in a high fever, and whatever time it was she had to get up.

It was five to four by her watch, too early to start the day, but after a cup of tea she might begin to feel sleepy again, and she put on shoes and dressing gown. Sam went ahead of her when she opened the door, trotting down the corridor towards his old room, and after a moment Felicity followed. She didn't want him scratching the door to get in, or barking and waking David, who must surely be back and asleep by now.

But when she turned the corner she saw the thread of light round the door which meant that David wasn't sleeping either. Perhaps he was working or reading, or just restless as she was, and she took a couple of steps forward before she checked herself. If she brought tea with her it wouldn't look so blatant. 'I was getting myself a drink,' she'd say, 'and I saw your light.' She crept along the passage and grabbed Sam's collar and he came without protest, allowing himself to be dragged away and following her down the stairs.

While she waited for the kettle to boil she went to the bar and took down two large tumblers. They had experimented with the recipe for Captain's Punch, and now she poured lime and lemon and stiff measures of Jamaican rum, adding hot water and spooning in sugar. Two cups of tea and two glasses of punch. 'I wasn't sure which you'd prefer,' she would say. 'Just take whatever it is you want.'

She was warm, glowing under the dressing gown and the cotton nightdress, and deep inside her nervous laughter began to bubble. She was risking another rejection. He might turn her away, but he might admit that he wanted her and it was too good a chance to miss, both of them awake in the dead of night and the house empty. She had to go to him.

She looked at herself in a mirror before she picked up the tray. Excitement was making her eyes sparkle and her cheeks flame. Her hair tumbled loose and she was breathing fast and she thought, This is it. If he shuts the door on me tonight I shall never find the courage to try again.

The light was still burning and her lips were trembling and she had started to shake. She bit hard on her underlip and knocked, softly at first and then, after a few seconds, louder. He must be asleep. Perhaps he hadn't bothered to get out of bed to switch off the light, but having come this far she would carry in the tray and say, 'I saw the light and thought you were awake.'

The door wasn't locked, but there was no one in the bed. Felicity stood in the middle of the room looking around. The main light was burning, so she could see at a glance that there was no one anywhere, and she realised that she must have left it on herself when she was in here earlier. David was spending the night somewhere else. Very likely with somebody else. Very likely Deirdre, and Felicity was going to spend the rest of the night torturing herself with images.

She turned off the light and took the tray back to her own room. She climbed into her own bed and gulped down both glasses of punch. By the time she was choking on the dregs of the second tears were pouring down her cheeks, but almost at once her head began to swim and she buried her face in the pillow and fell into a drugged slumber.

When she woke it was time to get up, but she must

have gone on crying in her sleep, because her head was heavy and the pillow was damp, and her reflection in the bathroom mirror sent her rushing to the kitchen for ice cubes from the fridge. She had to get the puffiness down, and she worked frantically with cold compresses, finally applying skin toner. Even then she needed careful make-up, but when that was finished she felt that she could blame it on a head cold if anybody remarked on her appearance.

This was the first time she had cried herself to sleep for a man in another woman's arms, and although she swallowed a couple of aspirins with a strong cup of coffee she still couldn't make herself take morning coffee up to the Captain's Room. It wouldn't make any difference whether David was there now or not. She couldn't face him yet, and say, 'Good morning,' and act naturally. Not yet.

He hadn't come down when Mrs Clemo arrived, and she was the one who went up to his room and returned to say that his bed hadn't been slept in.

Felicity said, 'Oh, I remember, he went out last night, he must have stayed with friends,' and Mrs Clemo accepted that, without realising that Felicity would have given an eye tooth to have known it was true.

When David did return, around midday, he brought a tall dark-haired woman with him, slick and smart in navy suit and scarlet topcoat, and introduced her to Felicity as, 'Mrs Armstrong, who'd like to see your accounts.'

Seeing them walk in together had seared Felicity. Mrs Armstrong could have been in her forties, but she was very attractive, and Felicity hoped that Mr Armstrong was still around.

David had said yesterday that a lawyer would be drawing up an agreement for Felicity to sign, and as

Mrs Armstrong took off her coat and settled down at the desk in the Captain's Room, with books and bills and quotes in front of her, Felicity asked, 'Are you a solicitor?'

'I'm an accountant. My husband's the solicitor. We're old friends of David's—and do call me Bella.' That was when Felicity decided that Bella Armstrong had one of the nicest smiles, and she smiled back and hurried to fetch her a pot of coffee. David had left again as soon as he'd seen the two women heading for the account books, and Felicity was busy around the house, looking into the Captain's Room after half an hour or so to ask if there were any questions.

'It all seems straightforward.' Bella Armstrong was wearing horn-rimmed spectacles now that she pushed up into her hair. 'David told us he's invested in your guest-house, and it seems a charming place.' Felicity warmed to her even more. 'So it's just a question of deciding a fair rate of repayment, isn't it?'

'That's right.' She would work and *work*, but there was always an element of risk, and she said slowly, 'I hope the interest won't be too tough.'

'Oh, I'm sure you know David better than that.'

'Not all that well,' Felicity admitted.

'But I thought——' Bella smiled. 'Did I get the wrong impression? He phoned us last week and said he was bringing you over to meet us—we live in Padstow—and we thought he sounded——' she left it at that and, Felicity said,

'There's a girl called Deirdre Osborne.'

A guarded look appeared on Bella's face. 'A very beautiful girl,' she said.

'Isn't she? She's here, staying in a hotel.' Bella made no comment and Felicity had to add, 'I'm sure David has hordes of girl-friends,' then Bella laughed,

'Well, he's rarely without one, although they all find out sooner or later that he's a dyed-in-the-wool bachelor.' She indicated the account books. 'But this is just a business deal?'

'Oh yes,' as she kept telling everyone. She didn't want it that way, but it was. Bella adjusted her spectacles back on her nose.

'And you must have discussed terms with David?' They had. Originally he had offered an interest-free loan for as much as she needed, but that was a long time ago and everything had changed, and she said,

'He said he'd get someone to work out what I should be able to pay each month.'

'That sounds reasonable.' Bella smiled. 'And you're not likely to try cheating him, are you?' In spite of the smile Felicity wondered how much David had told the Armstrongs last night, arranging for Bella to come here with him this morning. She *was* a cheat in David's eyes. He would watch that she didn't dodge her debts. If she tried he would probably bankrupt and break her, and of course she wouldn't. She wasn't a fool, and she was honest, but all she could do now was force a smile, as if Bella had been joking, and perhaps she had, and change the subject by asking, 'You will stay for lunch?'

'Thank you, but I have to get back.'

'Can I give you a lift? I don't know where David is.' He might turn up before Bella was through here, or he could still be around the cove, but Bella said,

'I've got my car. David met me this morning in the car park.'

'So he wasn't——' Felicity bit back the words, 'he wasn't with you and your husband last night,' and gulped and got out, 'Has he invited you to our opening, Saturday week?'

'We're looking forward to it,' said Bella.

In the next few days Felicity began to wonder if she was getting out of her depth. Of course she wanted publicity. She wanted her guest-house to be a success, but plans for the opening seemed very ambitious.

The guests who were coming because David had asked them ranged from an actor-knight, who had a palatial home just along the coast, to an international beauty queen who was rarely out of the gossip columns. The press, local and farther afield, would be here in force, and so would Felicity's friends and customers, including most of Trevarrow's Yard and Edward Cunliffe.

David was footing the bill for the buffet, a flowing bowl of Captain's Punch and a glass of celebration champagne for each guest, and slightly, sometimes, Felicity was beginning to panic. Nobody agreed with her. Even Mrs Clemo couldn't see what could go wrong, except possibly the weather. They were ready to re-open, the house had never looked better, and if business did pick up in future Jessie would be helping with the cooking—Jessie was as good a cook as Felicity—and several local girls would be happy to be offered jobs as waitresses or chambermaids.

'Look,' said Felicity, 'it's never going to be a four-star hotel,' and Mrs Clemo said they knew that, but Felicity had been the one who had been so keen to put Gull Rock House on the tourist map, so pleased that somebody as well known as David Holle was backing her, so what was worrying her now?

She shouldn't have been worried. She had signed the agreement and she ought to be able to meet the terms, but she couldn't help wondering what David would do if she couldn't pay. She saw very little of him. Most evenings he was out and most days he was working in his room. She heard the clacking of his typewriter and sometimes took in his meals. When he saw her he could totally ignore her if he was working, or he could be pleasant enough if they passed in a corridor or met downstairs. But he never stayed to talk, and when Felicity tried to discuss arrangements for Saturday he said, 'It's all yours. I've done all I'm doing, and good luck.'

'Will Deirdre be coming?' She was hurting herself, not him, she wasn't even annoying him.

'No.'

'Will you?'

'Of course,' and he walked out of the lounge into the open air and she wished he had never come here. Things hadn't been so bad, she was making a living. She had had Gordon and the future might have been as good as most people's lives. But she was lying to herself because, even if David had forgotten, she could never in her heart wish away the time when they had come so near to being lovers.

And it seemed he had not forgotten. Early Thursday morning, two days before the opening party, Felicity in her nightgown walked into a bathroom as David stepped out of the shower. 'Get out!' he roared at her, clutching a towel round his waist, and she shrieked, 'Why didn't you lock the door?'

'The latch must be faulty.'

His hair was dripping wet and his arms and chest gleamed and Felicity stared at the ugly scar, livid against the brown skin of his left shoulder. It didn't look like the kind of gash that glass would make, nor as though it dated from his boyhood, and she asked, '*Was* it a cold frame?'

'What?'

'The scar.'

'No,' he said. 'It was a sniper in Yamit.'

She whispered through dry lips, 'But you told Deirdre——'

'I didn't tell Deirdre unpleasant stories.' No, thought Felicity, neither would I. Deirdre had never had the stamina for facing reality, she would always need shielding and protecting. She croaked, 'You could have been *killed*!'

'But I wasn't.' He was so alive that she felt the warmth of him like the sun all over her, and it was the hardest thing not to take those few steps and throw her arms around him and burst into tears. 'Now do you mind getting out,' he said. 'I'm not forgetting how close I came to making a right bloody fool of myself over you.'

'How close did you come?' She ached for him to touch her and tell her, but he didn't touch her. He told her,

'You nearly got the Turner, gift wrapped, for a start. And to cap that I was about to ask you to marry me.'

'They all find out sooner or later that he's a dyed-in-the-wool bachelor,' Bella had said, but he was going to ask Felicity to marry him, and that filled her with a terrible feeling of loss.

'Luckily,' he said, 'I had it spelled out for me that I needed a wife like you like a hole in the head—so, out!' He shoved her with a flat hand, sending her backwards, slamming the door, and she sagged against the wall in the corridor, her mind reeling.

David was adamant that he had no feeling for her now, but only a few days ago he had wanted her as his wife, and if his emotions had been that strong then there had to be something left, beyond cynical indifference. Some of the magic. It had been a kind of magic from the beginning. Like the sea-witch story. He had said he knew how Willie felt when he found his sea-witch, and he had painted Felicity as Carlotta.

I could be Carlotta on Saturday, she thought. I could dress like her and do my hair the same way and wear the seed-pearl brooch.

He had been going to ask her to marry him, surely there was hope in that; and she wouldn't let herself consider that if he had cared less it might have been easier, that because he had come so close to offering so much in future his pride would keep him for ever on guard against her.

Saturday morning dawned sullen but calm. The skies were grey, it could start raining, but there were no gale warnings and no charted storms heading for Tregorran Cove, so the guests should have no difficulty navigating the improved causeway and reaching Gull Rock House.

Inside the house preparations continued on the buffet, and just after midday Edward Cunliffe turned up. When Felicity came down the stairs he was in the middle of the lounge talking to Mrs Clemo, and she hurried across to them smiling, 'Mr Cunliffe—I'm *so* glad you could make it!'

He had been blinking through his spectacles, at the painting of the sea-witch, at the new brightness of everything, and when he saw Felicity the blinking intensified. She was still in a scarlet sweater and a denim skirt at this stage, but she was in a high state of nervous tension like an actress in the wings, eyes very bright, generating excitement. She couldn't stand still and it was hard to stop chattering. 'What do you think of us?' she asked him.

'Very nice,' said Mr Cunliffe, who had asked her the

last time he was here to call him Edward. He looked from Felicity to the painting above the fireplace. He had read the leaflet and knew about Carlotta now. 'I never realised,' he went on, 'that you were descended from a sea-witch, but let me say it does not surprise me. I have always considered you a bewitching lady.'

She thanked him and took him up to his room, and he was impressed by that too. Then he came down again and was served with lunch, while Felicity took a tray in to David and said, 'One of the guests has come—Edward Cunliffe.'

There was a time when David had said he wanted to meet Edward, but now he said, 'Put it down there, would you?' meaning the tray, and went on scowling at the typewriter and banging the keys.

Half past six was the time that Gull Rock House was officially declared open, but half an hour before that the folk from Trevarrow's Yard started to arrive. The ones who had worked on the guest-house face-lift felt personally involved, and they were friends and this was a celebration and they were here to support Felicity.

Her costume was a great success. She was in a Laura Ashley dress that had the same high neckline as the painting, the seed-pearl brooch pinned at the throat, long sleeves and long skirt; and after a little practice she had twined her hair in a coronet with tendrils falling alluringly. When she stood under the painting she could have been the model for it. 'You should be holding a shell,' said the girl who had made the patchwork quilts, and Felicity said, 'Oh, I do, I do, but I've just put it down for the moment. Oh, hello, Gordon.'

Gordon was early too. He had had some idea of catching Felicity on her own for a few minutes and was annoyed to find her surrounded by a small crowd. He told her she looked charming and that he was sure the

evening would be most enjoyable, and he hoped——
He didn't say what he hoped, but he looked around
with an expression that said he was pretty sure she was
riding for a fall. Then he sat down in a corner and
Felicity went to find Margie and begged, 'Please look
after Gordon. He isn't happy about this.'

'You surprise me,' said Margie, and laughed.

When the cars started appearing along the quayside
Felicity knocked on David's door. 'Come in,' he called.
He was still typing at the desk and she said, 'They're
probably your guests arriving. Most of the ones I know
are here.'

'I didn't know it was fancy dress.' She didn't feel like
a bewitching lady, she felt like a lady who was going to
make a fool of herself.

'Please come down,' she said. 'The press will be here,
all sorts of people. I need you.'

'You need nobody.' But he got up. 'I didn't expect
you to get stage fright. What do you think's going to
happen down there?'

'My friends have hearty appetites and there isn't
much money in arts and crafts. They've started on the
buffet. We could have a bare board by the time Sir Leo
Lansing arrives.' David burst out laughing,

'He's overweight anyway, and there's plenty of food.
All you're facing tonight are a few well-wishers, and
that's no great ordeal.'

To wish her luck with her guest-house, and she could
have dealt with that. It would have been fun, easy.
Felicity wondered what he would have said if she'd told
him, 'I'm dressed like this for you. Because my last
hope is that you'll find me bewitching, and I don't think
I care about the house any more. I care about you, only
you, and if you held out a hand I'd go with you, right
out of that door, and never look back.'

She was following him, to the top of the stairs. As they came down somebody shouted, 'Give us a smile!' and David slipped an arm round her shoulders and a light flashed. The press were here. David steered Felicity to them and she said what she hoped were the right things, and there were enough celebrities around to ensure plenty of publicity coverage.

Sir Leo Lansing said he could heartily recommend the Captain's Punch, and as he was playing Falstaff that season a picture of him with a tankard in his hand made a good shot. A famous gourmet-journalist said the food was excellent, and a gorgeous girl who was appearing in a TV series said someone had given her one of Felicity's sea-spells before she went for the audition that got her the part. Felicity wasn't sure whether to believe that or not. She suspected it could have been David's suggestion, especially as the girl spent a lot of time talking to him.

He had glamorous friends. It seemed to Felicity that all the time he was surrounded, and at least one woman was hanging on to him. She herself talked with Bella for a while and was invited over to Padstow. 'When you have the time,' said Bella. 'It's a shame David can't bring you, but he's moving on soon, isn't he?'

'Sure to be,' said Felicity, and her heart felt like lead in her chest. He had stayed to finish his script, and probably to see tonight through, because he had a stake in the guest-house and tonight should get it off to a good start. There wouldn't be any reason for him to stay afterwards.

'I think this place is thrilling,' the TV starlet gushed at Felicity. 'And this is really the anniversary that she came, with the storm raging and everything?'

'Right,' said David. 'About now, I should think.' It was getting late, time to open the champagne and call it a night. They brought out the bottles and the corks began popping, and the photographers posed Felicity and David under the painting of Carlotta.

'A toast to the sea-witch,' Arthur Penrose proclaimed, and in the moment of silence, while everybody sipped, somebody shouted,

'I'll tell you what she is! It's not a sea-witch, it's a wrecker. They were wreckers along here, it's wrecker coast, and that's what her family must have been. And I'm warning you, Holle, or whatever your name is, she's a taker. You'll get nothing back from her, nothing!'

Incredibly it was Gordon, looking so flushed and belligerent that Felicity hardly recognised him, and when Edward Cunliffe, standing near, ventured a mild protest, 'I say, that's not very——' Gordon took a swing at him, sending him lurching against Sir Leo, who went sprawling, taking several others down with him, to a chorus of shrieks and shouts.

It was a chaotic scene. Gordon flailing around, Edward Cunliffe searching for his spectacles, dishevelled guests, and, of course, the photographers clicking away in all directions. Felicity froze. Gordon must have gone raving mad, and with all these camera shots Gull Rock House would probably make the nationals and get itself a reputation that meant that anyone with any sense at all would avoid it like the plague.

All she could do was watch, so numb with shock that from then on everything seemed in slow motion. Guests were brushing themselves down. Margie had Gordon by the lapels of his jacket and was hissing at him and backing him towards a chair, into which he collapsed. David was talking to Sir Leo, who seemed to have come to no harm, and three reporters were asking Felicity who Gordon was.

'A friend,' she said. 'I thought.'

'Not as good a friend as David Holle?' It had been emphasised that David Holle's interest here was purely business, but a jealous lover running berserk was a lively angle, and Felicity's blood ran cold as she stammered, 'I think the punch went to his head. I don't think he knew what he was saying.'

It brought the evening to a close, as everyone realised it was time they went. 'I'm so sorry,' said Margie, 'but you said to keep him happy and I kept filling his glass. I didn't know he had a weak head. Quite a turn, wasn't it?' She mimicked, ' "Wrecker country, this is." We'll get him home, he's in no state to drive.'

Gordon would probably wake in the morning with a raging hangover, and Felicity hoped he would, because he could have sabotaged her family trade for the season. Everybody looked cheerful when they went, but she could have wept, and she was sure David was furious, although he didn't show it. He said goodnight to the guests, and he suggested that the clearing up could wait till morning. When she was left with just Jessie and Mrs Clemo, and Jessie's husband Jan, Felicity felt so wrung out that she was incapable of making even a simple decision like that.

Edward Cunliffe and the others who were staying the night had gone to their rooms, except David, and Felicity looked at Mrs Clemo and Jessie and said, 'It was awful, wasn't it?'

Mrs Clemo was tight-lipped with disapproval, Jessie shrugged helplessly, and Jan looked worried for them all.

'Going on like that in front of everybody!' said Mrs Clemo. 'You've never taken anything from him. What's he ever done for you, except sell your knicknacks? I don't know what got into him.'

'The punch got into him,' said Jan. 'Will it get into the papers?' He was asking David, who said,

'The pictures will. There's nothing I can do about that.'

'Fighting and brawling!' snorted Mrs Clemo. 'Fine sort of name it'll give us!' Then she relented, seeing Felicity's distress. 'Only be a nine-day wonder, and it's as well you've seen the spiteful side of him. I've no patience with a man drinking if he can't hold his liquor.'

Jessie gave Felicity a comforting hug and promised to return early in the morning, then Felicity stood at the door to watch them go, by the light of the moon, across the causeway. David was standing by the fireplace, a glass in his hand, when she turned back. A muscle twitched by his mouth and she begged, 'Please don't be angry, I can't take any more.'

'Sir Leo could have sued us. Suppose he'd put his back out—and you know how easy that is to do.' He was being sarcastic, she supposed, but she asked,

'He won't, will he?'

'He's all right, and if he wasn't nothing would stop him from playing Falstaff.' David didn't sound angry, nor sarcastic. He was actually smiling, and although Felicity said dolefully,

'It *was* awful, all of them falling around,' her lips curved, and when he began to laugh she heard her own weak giggle. There was nothing to laugh at, except that she was holding back tears and laughter was another release. But having started it was hard to stop, and she wondered if she was hysterical, laughing until the tears came. She said at last, 'It won't do the business any good, but I'm beginning to feel sorry for Gordon. He's going to be shattered when he sobers up and realises what a performance he gave. I don't suppose he's ever raised his voice in public before.'

'He didn't sound like a man who'd had much practice,' said David. 'You need somebody who can raise his voice, in public and private, as often as it's necessary.'

'You agreed with what he said, though, didn't you?' That was what hurt most, that David shared Gordon's opinion of her. Somebody coughed at the top of the stairs and Edward Cunliffe came down, still fully dressed. Maybe *he's* going to sue me, Felicity thought wildly, and asked anxiously, 'Are you all right—can I get you anything?'

'I was concerned about you, the way the evening ended,' said Edward Cunliffe, still blinking behind his spectacles. 'I thought I'd just stress again that I shall continue to come here, and I'm sure that most of your clientele will. What happened just now isn't the sort of thing that happens often, is it?'

'Certainly not,' said David. 'You can't expect the chance to knock down Sir Leo Lansing every night!'

Edward laughed nervously. He had spoken up for Felicity and nearly had his glasses smashed for his trouble. Fortunately they had landed in the remains of a sherry trifle, and the whole thing had been surprisingly exhilarating. If he had found Felicity alone down here he might have told her how much he admired her, but David's Holle's presence stopped him doing that, so he wished them both goodnight and climbed the stairs again, while David strode off towards the dining room.

When Edward Cunliffe had vanished Felicity said, 'It was nice of him to come down and tell me he doesn't believe I'm running a disorderly house.'

'Put this on.' David was carrying a coat that had been hanging in the kitchen, and Sam, who had been shut in the kitchen most of the evening, was scratching at the front door. 'Let's take the dog for a walk,' said David. 'I want to talk to you and there's always the risk of another admirer coming down to offer condolences.'

Felicity didn't think it likely, and David wasn't jealous, she wasn't fooling herself about that. It had to be business talk, but the cool air and the wide vista of sea and sky were a pleasant change. There were stars in the sky and slow drifting clouds. The tide was out and the beach shimmered.

She had expected to stroll along the causeway, but David turned off it to climb down the rocks on to the beach, holding a hand out to her. This time she took his hand. Last time she had laughed and avoided his touch, and she wondered now how much was antagonism and how much, even then, a deep subconscious fear that this man's touch could light a fire.

He loosened her fingers when they reached the shingle and Sam, missing them on the causeway, came slithering down the rocks and loped off along the beach. Then David answered her question, as though there had been no interruption by Edward Cunliffe and she had only just asked it, 'No, I didn't believe what Gordon said.'

Felicity gasped. Did he mean that? Had he heard Gordon saying what she had heard, 'That I'm a taker, who gives nothing? You don't believe it? But I thought——'

'I know, but when somebody said it it sounded ridiculous. Of course there were no grounds for it. It was laughable.'

He wasn't laughing. They were walking now, Sam running. The beach was deserted with only the sound of the sea and overhead a moving pattern of clouds. She said, 'Deirdre must have gone on saying it.'

'Not to me. She went back to the South of France.'

'When?'

'Soon after she came.'

So there had been no Deirdre, all these days and nights. 'I thought you were spending most of your nights with her,' she said.

'Of course not.' She wished he would stand still so that she could concentrate on this. She wanted to stare into his face, but the shingle was soft underfoot and she was stumbling along, getting only side glances at a profile. 'She's a stunning looking girl,' he said, 'and I hope she does find a man who'll carry her for the rest of her life, but it's not me.'

Any more than Felicity could have promised the rest of her life to Gordon ... David went on, 'I stayed talking to her till late that first night, persuading her to go back. She was settling down happily it seems, until somebody told her they'd read that I was at Gull Rock House. When I left her I drove up the coast and sat looking at the sea and trying to get things straight.'

He turned to face the sea now. They had reached a rock outcrop and Felicity sat down, because that might stop him striding off again and because her legs were feeling weak. She looped her hands over her knees and listened, hardly breathing.

'It all seemed obvious then,' said David. 'You'd taken me for a mug and I'd bought it to the extent of falling in love for the first time in my life. But I thought I was tough enough to weather it. That I could even stay here and work on the script, and during the days it wasn't too hard. But the nights were bad. I kept away from the house most nights because I couldn't trust myself to keep away from your door. Or, if the door was unlocked, your bed.'

He was looking away from her, over the black water where the village slept under the waves. 'I stayed at the

Grand in Fenmouth most nights,' he said, and Felicity had nearly gone there, and if she had she would have found him alone and learned that Deirdre had left. She asked,

'Do you remember the last time we walked here, that first morning?'

'Of course.'

'I'm sorry I let you put money into the place.'

'You couldn't have stopped me. I'd have done it somehow as soon as I saw how much the place mattered to you.'

'I did hurt my back,' she told him, and he smiled at her.

'I believe you.'

'If I hadn't it would have been different.' They would have made love, admitted they were in love, and the misunderstandings would not have loomed so large when Deirdre came. 'But you might have tried,' she said. 'You never even stroked my hair. The whole fortnight you never laid a finger on me.'

He laid a finger on her now, but gently, sitting beside her on the rock, putting an arm around her, tilting her chin so that she looked up into his eyes and told her, 'I might not have been able to stop at stroking your hair, and I was afraid of hurting you. I could have made you want me, I thought you did, but with you it had to be right in every way. You were so special it had to be so right.'

She said huskily, 'If Gordon hadn't created that scene would you have gone away without telling me any of this?'

'I don't know.' He looked at her steadily and her heart was in her throat. 'I might have done, but I'd have come back. I got a gut reaction when I heard him say you gave nothing. You're brave and warm and beautiful, and as soon as I was away from you I should have realised that I'd lost every last lovely thing that made life worth living. I'd have been back, and I'd have stayed until you said that you'd come with me.'

He didn't know that she would go now, anywhere he asked her. His lips caressed her hair and he said, 'I think it was tonight that the sea-witch came.'

'So do I.'

'How long do you think it took William to teach her to love him?'

'No time at all, I should think.'

'Will you come with me?' She nodded and he said, 'Be careful. You know what you're promising?' He held her left hand so that she felt his touch like a ring on her finger, and she said with a flash of mischief,

'Do you know what you're taking on? My grandfather said I could call up the storm.'

'There's a lot to be said for a good storm.'

One other thing she had to say. 'Remember saying that I had to be frigid or a very determined virgin?' He remembered. 'There was a third explanation,' she said. 'That I was afraid of loving you too much.'

She heard his breath catch. 'Oh, darling,' he groaned, 'you'll never know what hearing you say that means to me!' His mouth covered hers and his lips were cold from the sea-mist, but the warmth of his kiss spread through her veins like liquid fire.

'Take me home,' she whispered, and he lifted her to her feet and they walked, linked and close, because home was in his arms, in his heart. Home was where they would be together, through the days and the nights and the years. Starting with tonight.

Harlequin® Plus

A WORD ABOUT THE AUTHOR

Jane Donnelly was born and raised in England. Trained as a journalist, she worked as a reporter on the local newspaper in a village on the edge of the Cotswolds, not far from Birmingham. After the birth of her daughter, she became the television critic for the *Birmingham Gazette*.

She was widowed when her daughter was only five and moved from her beloved village to Lancashire in the north. It was there that she began writing fiction—short stories, thrillers and movie scripts. When her daughter was in her teens, Jane attempted her first full-length book. She loved the experience—and so did her publisher—and continues to write warmhearted romances...almost fifteen years after the publication of *A Man Apart* (Romance #1227).

Jane returned to her former home in the Cotswolds when she learned that a certain historic house, a picture-perfect setting for writers, was for sale. She believes that her "cottage" is under some sort of happy magical spell. "After all," she says, "animals immediately make themselves at home here, and in the garden everything grows lushly!"

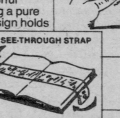

Great old favorites...
Harlequin Classic Library

The **HARLEQUIN CLASSIC LIBRARY** is offering some of the best in romance fiction— great old classics from our early publishing lists.

Complete and mail this coupon today!

Harlequin Reader Service

In U.S.A. 1440 South Priest Drive
Tempe, AZ 85281

In Canada 649 Ontario Street
Stratford, Ontario N5A 6W2

Please send me the following novels from the Harlequin Classic Library. I am enclosing my check or money order for $1.50 for each novel ordered, plus 75¢ to cover postage and handling. If I order all nine titles at one time, I will receive a FREE book, *Doctor Bill*, by Lucy Agnes Hancock.

☐ 109 **Moon over the Alps**
Essie Summers

☐ 110 **Until We Met**
Anne Weale

☐ 111 **Once You Have Found Him**
Esther Wyndham

☐ 112 **The Third in the House**
Joyce Dingwell

☐ 113 **At the Villa Massina**
Celine Conway

☐ 114 **Child Friday**
Sara Seale

☐ 115 **No Silver Spoon**
Jane Arbor

☐ 116 **Sugar Island**
Jean S. MacLeod

☐ 117 **Ship's Doctor**
Kate Starr

Number of novels checked @ $1.50 each =	$ _____
N.Y. and Ariz. residents add appropriate sales tax	$ _____
Postage and handling	$ ___.75
TOTAL $ _____	

I enclose _____
(Please send check or money order. We cannot be responsible for cash sent through the mail.)

Prices subject to change without notice.

Name _____
(Please Print)

Address _____
(Apt. no.)

City _____

State/Prov. _____ Zip/Postal Code _____

Offer expires December 31, 1983.

30656000000